groucho Marx, PRIVATE EYE

Also by Ron Goulart

Groucho Marx, Master Detective

groucho Marx, PRIVATE EYE

Ron Goulart

St. Martin's Press
New York

THOMAS DUNNE BOOKS.
An imprint of St. Martin's Press.

Production Editor: David Stanford Burr

Library of Congress Cataloging-in-Publication Data

Goulart, Ron.
    Groucho Marx, private eye / Ron Goulart.
       p.   cm.
    ISBN 0-312-19895-7
    1. Marx, Groucho, 1891–1977—Fiction. I. Title.
PS3557.O85G77   1999
813'.54—dc21   98-41752
                                    CIP

First Edition: April 1999

10 9 8 7 6 5 4 3 2 1

For Shirley Meech, a friend who actually reads my stuff

groucho Marx,
PRIVATE EYE

One

Groucho Marx played detective again in the spring of 1938.

The second murder case that he set out to solve came along in the nick of time. The investigation that we undertook, he later claimed, quite probably distracted him from committing a murder himself.

The object of Groucho's contemplated homicide was a plump, freckled teenager who was blighting our lives that April. A nasty, mean-minded kid, known to movie audiences as Polly Pilgrim, she loathed Groucho and despised me. As Groucho frequently pointed out, she didn't loathe him half as much as he loathed her. "That unnatural child," he told me, "combines all the best qualities of Typhoid Mary, Ma Barker, and Louis B. Mayer."

Unfortunately Polly was the new costar of our radio show.

The show, now heard every Thursday night over the Nationwide Broadcasting Network, had taken on a new sponsor and a modified title. Our original sponsor had cancelled on us at the end of 1937. After a short hiatus, though, we returned to the air and changed our title from *Groucho Marx, Master Detective* to *Groucho Marx, Private Eye*. Instead of selling Orem Bros.

Coffee our commercials were now peddling Mullens Pudding, whose snappy slogan was "It Comes in Five Flavorful Flavors." Later on I'll probably get around to listing all five of the flavors, but I can assure you now that, even though Groucho always insisted otherwise, herring was not one of them.

Groucho was still starring as private detective J. Hawkshaw Transom and I was still writing the scripts. But Polly, at the insistence of old Colonel Mullens himself, had been added to the cast to play Groucho's daughter Tippsy Transom. The Colonel, even after sitting through her movie performances in both *A Girl, a Guy and a Symphony* and *That Brat Is Here Again*, was convinced that she was destined to be another Deanna Durbin or Judy Garland. "If it was up to me," observed Groucho, "that midget Valkyrie would be destined, rather, for a long stay at either Devil's Island or Omaha, Nebraska."

Groucho and I had agreed to stay with the show despite Polly Pilgrim, mostly because of the money. MGM hadn't extended the Marx Brothers contract after *A Day at the Races* had been released in the spring of the previous year. Zeppo, now an agent, convinced RKO to hire his three brothers for a one-shot deal. The initial money was very good, but after Groucho had read the script of *Room Service* he became convinced that the picture, even though his old friend Morrie Ryskind had worked on the screenplay, would not only never show a profit but might well finish the careers of the Marx Brothers. "It very probably will also end the careers of the Smith Brothers, the Wright Brothers, and the Brothers Karamazov along with it," he told me. "The thing would have to be greatly improved before you could even call it lousy. In fact, I understand a rustic off in Wisconsin someplace wants to use the script, once we're through with it, as the cornerstone of a vast turkey farm." While waiting for the cameras to roll over at the RKO studios, he concentrated on our radio show.

I'm Frank Denby, by the way. I'd been a crime reporter on the *Los Angeles Times* for five years, but at this point I was a radio scriptwriter. I met Groucho in the summer of 1937 when he'd picked me to turn out the scripts for his show. That autumn, when he turned amateur sleuth for the first time, I worked with him on solving the murder of a young actress he'd once been friendly with. With my experience in police reporting and his natural instincts for detection, we'd made a pretty good team. I saw myself as being a sort of Archie Goodwin to his Nero Wolfe. "I never heard of this Archie Goodwin," he assured me. "I did know Archy the cockroach, however. And, I must tell you, Rollo, he was a much better writer than you are. Even though woefully lacking in capital letters."

In terms of things in general, 1938 wasn't any improvement over the previous year. People had barely stopped worrying about the Depression, when what was being called the Roosevelt Recession came along and unemployment jumped again to 20 percent. And by April you could feel World War II getting closer and closer. Japan was occupying more and more of China, Franco and his forces were doing increasingly well in the Spanish Civil War, and Hitler and the Nazis had already taken possession of Austria.

The new murder case actually got going on a windy Tuesday afternoon in Hollywood, although we didn't know it at the time. The rehearsal for Thursday night's broadcast was due to start in fifteen minutes and I was sitting up in the booth overlooking Studio C in the brand new NBN building on Sunset.

"Did you hear about that asshole dying?" inquired Annie Nicola, who was slumped in her chair, knees against the control panel, smoking a Kool cigarette.

"Be more specific," I suggested.

"The poor man's Ronald Colman. Brian Montaine, star of *The Sword of Charlemagne* and far too many other costume epics." Annie was our show director, a dark-haired thickset woman in her early forties. Today she was wearing white slacks and a shaggy pullover.

"Yeah, it was on Johnny Whistler's Hollywood gossip segment on KNX this morning." I eased up out of my seat and backed away just as she exhaled more mentholated smoke in my direction. "Understand Montaine was in the middle of a new movie."

"Yet another costume epic. *The Legend of King Arthur.*"

The only other person in the booth just then was our announcer, Harry Whitechurch. "Laugh if you will," he said in his deep, rich, jovial voice, "but Montaine was one hell of an actor. And, which is rare in this town, a swell guy, too." He sighed and the pages of the script he was holding fluttered. "That's a tough break, dying at thirty-seven of a heart attack."

"C'mon, despite what his studio bio claimed, that hambone was at least forty-five," Annie told him. "I remember seeing him in *Way Down East* back in the silents."

"Well, that's still damn young to be felled by a heart attack," said the hefty announcer.

I glanced down at the studio stage and noticed that Polly, in a pale blue party dress, was sitting in one of the folding chairs sadly reading the front page of the *Los Angeles Examiner.* The headline, I knew, was about Brian Montaine's sudden death.

Then I spotted Groucho. He'd entered at the rear of Studio C and was slouching along the center aisle between the rows of plush audience seats. "I better go head him off," I said, hurrying

4

for the door, "before he and Polly collide."

Groucho was wearing a lime green polo shirt, a plaid sport-coat, and slacks of a wheat-field brown. He had a dead cigar clenched between his teeth and his thinning hair was tousled.

"You look a mite windblown," I said, stepping into his path.

He halted, removed the unlit cigar from his mouth and eyed me. "I intend, and my press secretary will confirm this, to ignore an obvious setup line like that, young sir," Groucho informed me as he smoothed down his hair. "I'm wondering if I ought to mention that my press secretary isn't here at the moment because he's home pressing my other pair of good pants."

I shook my head. "I wouldn't, since the townspeople are already muttering about tar and feathers."

"Ah, but they've promised to use ostrich plumes for the feathers this time." He pointed a finger ceilingward. "And you know how fetching I always look in those. By Jove, Bunny, I've a mind to take them up on it."

Over her booth microphone Annie inquired, "Are you about ready to return to reality, Groucho, and consider starting our little rehearsal?"

Shielding his eyes with the cigar-holding hand, he hunched and squinted up at her. "We aren't due to return to reality until late next Tuesday, dear lady," he told our director. "For myself, and I can't speak for the rest of the expedition, I don't intend to return until I've seen the Pyramids. The last trip, as you may recall, the Pyramids were out of town and I was terribly disappointed. I was also terribly dressed, which accounts for their not giving us a table close to the Sphinx. They did seat us near the Finks, a delightful couple in spite of their poor bladder control, and it turned out to be just the bestest summer vacation Penrod and I ever had, teacher."

5

"You're the Gertrude Stein of comedy, Groucho," Annie assured him.

"Thanks, but I really don't think I'm masculine enough to stand in for Gertie." He suddenly dodged around me and went loping toward the stage.

Before I could catch up with him, he trotted up the side steps, went sprinting over to Polly, and lifted the newspaper free of her pudgy fingers.

"Oaf," she remarked, grabbing at it.

"I merely wish to borrow the funnies, Miss Borgia," Groucho explained. "I haven't perused *Barney Google* yet today and I'm eager to learn if—"

"Don't you know he's dead." Sniffling, she succeeded in snatching the *Examiner* out of his grasp.

Groucho rose up on his toes, looking stunned. "Barney Google is dead?" he said forlornly. "Gad, I saw him only yesterday and he looked simply lovely. I was, I have to admit, a trifle concerned about those googly eyes of his and suggested he see an oculist at once. Or, at the very least, an ocarina, which is a female oculist except in February. The point being—"

"It's Brian Montaine who's dead, you halfwit." Polly rolled the paper up and attempted to swat him with it. "And he was a better actor than you'll ever be."

Groucho bobbed clear of her swing. "Don't be too sure about that, Pollyanna. Not until you've seen *me* in a suit of armor."

"You're nothing but a cheap buffoon." She tried for another swat, but I, gently, caught her arm.

"What say," I suggested, "we call a truce?"

"This little whippersnapper has accused me of being a cheap buffoon." He inserted the cigar back between his teeth. "I'll have you know that I happen to be just about the most expensive buffoon in this man's town."

"Might we, Groucho, think about starting?" Margaret Dumont, who was playing our perennial dowager Mrs. Uppercase, had walked out onto the stage, script in hand.

"Maggie, my pet, you're a vision." He hurried over to her in bent-knee fashion and clutched her hand. After kissing it a few times, he let go and stepped back. "Just look at you, Miss Chloe. The last time I saw you, my dear, you were a mere slip of a girl and now—why, I declare, you're at least three slips, two girdles, four pairs of shorts, and one of those dojiggers that holds up stockings. My lands."

The rest of the cast, which included Hans Conreid, who was playing Inspector Sprudelwasser, and Rob Stolzer, who was Rosco the office boy, had arrived by now and were occupying the row of folding chairs.

Harry Whitechurch cleared his throat majestically and stepped up to one of the microphones.

"If you're through cavorting, Groucho," mentioned Annie from above, "we'll get going on this run-through."

"I haven't cavorted since I was eleven," he told her. "But, let's be truthful, if they hadn't caught me doing it out behind the barn I might be cavorting still."

Harry nodded at Groucho and grinned. He leaned into the mike and said, "Good evening, ladies and gentlemen. From the heart of Hollywood we present—Groucho Marx, Private Eye, starring none other than Groucho Marx. And brought to you by Mullens Pudding. Remember, it comes in five flavorful flavors. Chocolate, Vanilla, Butterscotch, Strawberry, and—"

"Herring," said Groucho as he shuffled over to his microphone.

Harry chuckled and then added, "Pistachio."

"I thought you could only eat pistachios in months with an *R* in them."

"Annie," piped up Polly.

"Yes, dear?"

"You were supposed to tell him."

"Tell him what, honey?"

"Not to make faces at me, but he's doing it already."

"Don't make faces at the kid, Grouch," suggested the director from behind the wide glass window of the booth.

He spread his hands wide and assumed a guileless look. "I swear to you, Annie, that my face froze this way on a recent trip to the icehouse. Alas, it's locked in an expression of deep revulsion, but that, I can assure one and all, has nothing whatsoever to do with that odious gnat yonder."

"Nertz." Polly stuck out her tongue at him.

"Might I suggest that both you adolescents stop this now," said Margaret Dumont.

"I apologize, Maggie." His apologetic bow was so deep that it caused him to bonk his head against the mike.

"Take it from the top again, Harry," said Annie, coughing out smoke.

We managed to get all the way through my script with only a few minor incidents. Midway in the show, on orders from Colonel Mullens, we had to insert what he referred to as "a musical interlude." That meant the comedy had to stop while Polly Pilgrim sang "a light opera favorite" each and every week.

Actually, she had a very good voice. I just didn't think it fit very well into a baggy pants show like ours.

Groucho had refrained from making faces at her or, as he sometimes did, tickling her while she was going for the high notes. But during her rendition of the "Indian Love Call" he did put his forefinger under his chin, roll his eyes, and stand on one foot in a cherublike pose when she came to the "calling you-oo-oo-oo-oo-oo-oo" part.

Polly quit in midsong, ran over and gave him a hearty kick in the ankle.

"Foul," cried Groucho as he began hopping around in a small circle.

The rehearsal wound up at a few minutes after five that afternoon and I hadn't the slightest notion that Groucho and I would soon be teamed again on a murder investigation.

And I sure didn't suspect who our client was going to be.

Two

The wind continued and the next day it was even stronger. At dusk it was vigorously rattling all the shutters on my beach cottage in the town of Bayside. As I stepped out of the house, the wind plucked a couple of loose shingles off the roof and sent them spinning and flapping down at me.

I dodged, hunched my shoulders, and started striding off along the darkening sands. On my right the twilight Pacific was gray and choppy. Grit and even little flecks of dead seaweed came flying through the air and somewhere unseen a small dog was howling forlornly.

After fighting the wind for nearly a mile, I reached Jane Danner's cottage and double-timed up to knock on her door.

She opened it, smiled out at me.

"I understand," I said, "that there's an oasis for rent someplace in these parts."

"This is the place." She took hold of both my hands and pulled me across the threshold.

Jane's living room is much better furnished than mine and always manages to look a lot cozier. I mentioned that just prior to kissing her.

The best-looking cartoonist in America, Jane is a slim young woman with reddish hair and I'd fallen in love with her the previous autumn. That happened on the same day Groucho invited me to become his colleague in amateur detection. All in all, it was a momentous day.

I'd better mention that there's not going to be much suspense in our romance. With us it was boy meets girl, boy stays with girl the rest of his life.

"Speaking of rentals." She moved away from me to settle on the sofa. "I made an appointment for us to see Mr. Farris tomorrow afternoon."

"That's the real estate guy?" I sat in her vicinity.

"Yes, and he's certain he can get us a much bigger beach place for less than the combined rents we're paying now."

"Great," I said. "What time?"

"Two."

"That'll be okay, sure. I don't have to get to the broadcast till five."

She studied my face for a few seconds. "You're absolutely sure that you want to go through with this?"

"Didn't I just fight my way through a sandstorm to be at your side?" I put my hand over hers. "Ma'am, I'd be right tickled to shack up fulltime with you."

"Be serious, huh?" she suggested.

"Golly, I try, but I keep flunking the entrance exam."

Jane managed to sigh and smile at the same time. "If you hadn't told me you'd been a smartass before you met Groucho," she observed, "I'd suspect you caught some kind of germ from him. You know, some bug that makes you hide your feelings behind funny remarks."

"You mean you think I've contracted Grouchoitis? I was

wondering why I've been walking with a pronounced slouch ever since last—"

"Frank."

"Okay," I conceded. "But seriously, I am perfectly happy about our living together fulltime in the same house."

"I mean about—"

"Not getting married before we move in together? I'd rather we did, but I understand why you—"

"I know it sounds goofy," she admitted. "Especially since you're the first man I've ever even really wanted to live with. But my parents got divorced when I was only—"

"Whoa." I held up my hand. "I feel it's time I told you that I'm not actually Sigmund Freud. He's out to lunch and I'm merely the guy who came in to reupholster his couch."

"All right." Smiling, she leaned back. "I promise never to be serious with you again, Frank."

"Yeah, but how can I be sure you're serious about that?"

She stood up, touching her fingertips to my cheek briefly. "Come into my studio."

Jane was working as assistant, sometimes ghost, to Rod Tommerlin. He turned out the successful rustic comic strip, *Hillbilly Willie*. At last count, it was running in a little under five hundred newspapers across the country. Days she worked at his house, but she also had a small studio here in her cottage.

She paused in the doorway, leaned against the jamb. "I haven't mentioned this project to you before," she told me. "Mainly because I wasn't sure if I could bring it off. Well, I did and now I really would like your honest opinion."

Nodding, I followed her into the small room. Like all the others, it was neat and orderly. There were two file cabinets along the left-hand wall, a drawing board, desk, and taboret in

13

the center of the room. On three of the walls she'd hung framed comic strip originals. My favorites were the hand-colored *Krazy Kat* Sunday page George Herriman had given her and a large self-portrait from Milt Gross.

There was a black leather portfolio resting on the slanted board. Smiling, a bit tentatively, she crossed over and opened it. "Take a look," she said. "And I really want, Frank, your *honest* opinion."

Jane spread out six original daily strips, then nodded for me to sit in the chair and look them over.

Each strip had the title *Hollywood Molly* lettered over the leftmost panel. Her drawings were great, done in a style that was all hers. They weren't in the broader manner she had to use when assisting Tommerlin on his moonshine extravaganza.

Molly was a pretty blonde, but smart, who'd just arrived in Hollywood to try to crash the movies. The writing was good, too, and the strip managed to be both funny and at the same time touching.

Okay, I know that sounds like a blurb provided by somebody who's in love with Jane. But *Hollywood Molly* really was a great comic strip.

I laughed, pushed back from the drawing board, and took her hand. "Jesus, this stuff is absolutely—"

The telephone rang out in the living room.

She ignored it. "Absolutely what?"

"Terrific," I told her as I hugged her. "Also stupendous, colossal, and not too bad. You can hand Tommerlin your resignation first thing tomorrow morning and—"

"I think I'll wait until I sell Molly." She pivoted and hurried into the next room to catch the phone.

"The strip is also monumental." I followed her out of the studio.

She picked up the phone from the coffee table. "Hello?" She glanced over at me, poked her tongue into her cheek. "Yes, he is here, Groucho. No, that won't be any need of that, since Frank already has his clothes on." She held the receiver out at arm's length.

"What, Groucho?" I inquired.

"Didn't I warn you about cohabiting with a lass who's as bright and intelligent as this one is, Rollo?" He was obviously puffing on a cigar as he spoke. "I was just recently reading an article in *The New England Journal of Medicine* that provided the dread news that intelligence may be contagious. So unless you drop her at once you're liable to lose your moron status, my lad. Think of what a handicap that would be in our business. For one thing, you'd never again be able to communicate with Colonel Mullens on his own level nor—"

"I neglected to tell you, sir, that I now take all my father-son lectures from Lewis Stone. Did you have any other rational purpose in phoning?"

"I did indeed," he continued. "How would you like to resurrect our once thriving detective business?"

"I wouldn't mind actually. When do we commence?"

"This very night, Rebecca," answered Groucho. "As a matter of fact, I have our newest client right here in the next room."

"So who the hell is it?"

"I'll give you a hint, Watso. What is it that's vile, loathsome, and even less fun than a really bad case of bubonic plague?"

"Surely, Groucho, you haven't got Polly Pilgrim under the

same roof with you?"

"Bingo," he said. "If you can curb your lust, I'd like you to speed over to my manse in that lemon yellow rattletrap of yours. Not only is the game afoot, Rollo, but my foot's a little gamy."

Three

All things considered, my yellow secondhand Plymouth coupé made pretty good time up into Beverly Hills. The harsh night wind buffeted the car, nearly shoving me clean off the road once. The imitation raccoon tail I'd never gotten around to detaching from the radio antenna flapped like a battle pennant all the way there.

When I turned onto the wide white gravel drive of Groucho's sprawling Moorish-style home on North Hillcrest Road, I noticed Polly's peach-colored limousine up near the garages.

I parked near it and slid free of my coupé.

Her chauffeur was sitting in the limo smoking a cigarette. He rolled the window a third of the way down, causing sparks to come flickering out into the darkness.

"Hiya, Frankie." He jerked a thumb in the direction of the house. "Brat's inside."

I gave him a grunt for a response, then headed for the doorway.

Groucho himself yanked the door open just as I was reaching for the knocker. "Thank goodness you're here, Dr. Kildare. We boiled plenty of hot water just like you told us on the phone," he said as he ushered me inside out of the windy night. "I'm afraid, though, that we got tired of waiting for you and converted most of the hot water into matzo ball soup. Could you, do you suppose, use the water anyway and just ignore the floating matzo balls and the lumps of chicken?"

"Where's Polly?"

"Oh, I know where *she* is—out in the kitchen." Groucho was wearing a smoking jacket that might have been in fashion back in the early 1920s and a pair of tweedy, and baggy, slacks. "It's the present whereabouts of my latest wife and my two adorably cute offspring I'm a trifle vague about. Though I'd guess Arthur is off playing tennis someplace, quite possibly a tennis court." He went loping off along the wide hallway.

I trailed after him. "Now would be a good time to tell what exactly is going on, Groucho?"

"For a fellow who once came this close to winning a Pulitzer for reporting, Rollo, you certainly haven't been keeping up with the latest news."

"I never came anywhere near a Pulitzer Prize all the while I was with the *LA Times.*"

"Ah, that may explain why you're a few murders behind. This story just broke officially about three hours ago. Newspapers haven't hit the stands with it yet, but I happened to hear it on the radio." He dived into his big yellow and white kitchen. "Look who's here, Pollyanna, my sweet. It's Uncle Franklin."

The freckled girl, much subdued, was sitting at the table, both pudgy hands circling a mug of cocoa. She was wearing a pink cardigan and tan slacks. It was obvious she'd been crying. "Good evening, Mr. Denby," she said in a quiet voice. "I'm awfully sorry to bother you and Mr. Marx like this, except I don't know anyone else I can . . ." She trailed off, slumped, and began crying softly.

I looked from her to Groucho, perplexed, frowning. "I get it," I said. "This quiet and courteous kid isn't really Polly, it's her stand-in."

"She's the true and authentic Polly Pilgrim," Groucho assured me. "Sit yourself and I'll explain the situation to you."

He took the chair next to hers and actually put a comforting arm around the shoulders of the young singer.

Still puzzled, I sat opposite the two of them. "Okay, so?"

"Drink the rest of your cocoa, kiddo," he advised the sniffling girl as he withdrew a crisp pocket handkerchief from his jacket and passed it to her.

Polly took it, dabbed at her puffy eyes, and then blew her nose. "Thank you, Mr. Marx." She held on to the handkerchief, squeezing it into a tight ball.

"All right, here's the setup," began Groucho. "Early today Dr. Russell Benninger, the noted Beverly Hills nose job artist, was found murdered in his beachfront mansion in Bayside."

Benninger had been a highly successful plastic surgeon and he'd remodeled many a famous aging face, male and female. Acting on an anonymous tip, the Bayside police, including our old antagonist Sergeant Branner, had entered the doctor's seaside home. They found him, in his pajamas, sprawled on the cream-colored carpet of the master bedroom. Between wives at the moment, Dr. Benninger was, officially anyway, living by himself.

He'd been shot twice in the head, at close range, with a .38 revolver.

Less than two hours later they'd arrested Polly's mother for the killing.

Let me give you some background on Polly's parents, since

that had a lot to do with why she was there in Groucho's kitchen crying. Polly's mother was the screen actress Frances London. A blonde in the Joan Blondell-Jean Harlow tradition, she had considerable success in the early thirties. For Paramount she starred in such box-office hits as *Blonde Tramp, Singapore Lady,* and *Bitter Bargain.* After that one, Frances went into a decline. Mostly it was drinking and, some said, drugs that did her in. She would fail to show up at the studio for filming, insult her directors, stumble on her lines over and over. And she got herself into several public scrapes, including one hit-and-run, a couple of shoplifting attempts, several disorderly conduct, and driving while under the influence of alcohol charges. The studio dumped Frances in 1934 and nobody else would hire her. She dropped from sight the next year, lived in a rooming house in the Bunker Hill area of LA and, again according to rumors, did just about anything to keep alive.

But about a year ago, after voluntarily committing herself to a church-run rehabilitation program, the actress reappeared. She no longer drank and, with the help of a second-string agent, got back into movies by the way of bit parts. A few weeks earlier she'd successfully auditioned for the role of the wife in MGM's upcoming series, *Dr. Dunn and Family.*

Polly had been born out of wedlock, but when Frances married Roger Pilgrim in 1930, he had legally adopted the girl. Pilgrim, a husky man in his fifties, came from a rich and conservative old California family. In recent years he'd become a partner in a public relations firm that specialized in the handling of the campaigns of some fairly conservative political candidates.

Pilgrim divorced Frances in 1934 and easily got custody of Polly. The child had an impressive singing voice and her father pushed her into an entertainment career. Polly got her first movie part when she was eleven. A gruff and distant man, Pilgrim didn't especially like his adopted daughter, but he treated her about as well as he treated anybody.

"My mother didn't kill that man," insisted Polly now, looking across at me.

"Why'd they arrest her then?"

Groucho said, "It's mostly circumstantial stuff, Frank."

The only fingerprints on the murder gun were those of Frances London. And most of the police departments in Greater Los Angeles had collected her prints in the days when she was a flamboyant drunk about town.

When the cops went to her small house in Manhattan Beach, they found the blond actress unconscious on the floor. She smelled strongly of booze and a subsequent test determined that her bloodstream contained considerably more than the legally allowed limit of alcohol. Polly's mother claimed she'd never been near Benninger's place, hadn't seen him for weeks.

"Wait now," I put in. "What was her relationship with him?"

"They were an item for several months," explained Groucho. "But Frances was certainly not the only lady in his busy social life. He seems to have been what is technically known as a tomcat."

"She quit seeing him," insisted Polly, grip tightening on the cup.

Groucho took out a fresh cigar and absently unwrapped it. "Unfortunately, Frances ran into Dr. Benninger by chance at the Trocadero a couple weeks ago. A shouting match followed and, according to those who were still sober enough to witness anything, there was physical violence on both sides. Some of them swear Frances threatened to bump the sawbones off because he'd

21

jettisoned her." He shrugged.

"That's just not true," insisted the young singer, sniffling and rubbing at her nose with the borrowed handkerchief.

I asked her, "Have you seen your mother since she was arrested?"

She nodded, snuffling. "I made my father let me go see her," she answered. "They've got her in a holding cell at the Bayside Police Department."

"What does she say about the cops finding her drunk?"

Polly took a slow deep breath. "She got a phone call last night from her agent," she said. "He told her a producer who was considering her to star in a series of B-movies about a girl reporter wanted to see her. She was supposed to go out to a private home over in Pasadena. But when she got into the hallway, someone hit her on the back of the head and she passed out."

"And?"

"That's all she remembers, Mr. Denby, until she woke up back in her house with the darn police standing all around her. She swears she hasn't taken a drink since she quit and she can't explain why she appeared to be drunk."

"It doesn't look good," I told Groucho.

"Gets better," he assured me. "Frances showed them a bump on her head, where she was bopped. Branner, of fond memory, said she wasn't sapped. She simply bumped her noggin when she fell down drunk."

"That's a lie, Mr. Marx. You can't go saying—"

"I'm just recounting the police view, kiddo," he explained. "While the sarge was there he got a call telling him that his men had found two witnesses who'd swear they saw Frances, staggering pretty thoroughly, approach the good doctor's door and pound on it. She yelled for him to open, promising if he didn't

22

she'd toss a brick through his goddamned window."

Polly tugged at his sleeve. "I know something else important," she said. "I saw a needle mark, red and inflamed on my mom's arm. Right here." She tapped a spot a few inches above her wrist."

"I know, you and your mother believe she was drugged and then somebody forced liquor down her," he said. "Trouble is, the cops will simply say she's using drugs as well as drinking."

Polly shook her head forcibly. "No, that's a damned lie, Mr. Marx," she insisted. "Since she stopped drinking—and stopped for good—my mother has never lied to me. She knows she's an alcoholic and can't take a drink for the rest of her life." She paused to inhale and exhale. "And the stuff about her ever taking drugs is just so much Hollywood bullshit."

"How often do you see her, Polly?" I asked.

"Since she got better, my father lets me visit her once a week," she answered. "I'll tell you this, too, I've been to her little house lots of times and there's never been a trace of liquor or anything else bad there. She hardly even smokes anymore, really."

Groucho lit the cigar with a wood match, took a few thoughtful puffs while contemplating the high white ceiling. "She got a lawyer?"

"Yeah, my father hired that oily shyster Ethan Cardwell."

"Caldwell is not only a shyster, dear child, he's the shyster's shyster," Groucho said. "But he's got a pretty good courtroom record."

"He wants my mother to plead innocent by reason of insanity."

Groucho pointed his cigar at me. "What do you think? Did Frances do it?"

23

"Her alibi is so lousy," I told him, "it's probably God's truth."

Groucho asked the girl, "Powder burns?"

Polly looked at her hands. "Yes, they did a paraffin test and it was positive," she admitted quietly. "But, don't you see, that has to be part of the frame up. I know it."

I said, "You haven't exhibited any especial fondness for Groucho or me, Polly. So why come to him now?"

"I read all about how you solved the murders of Tom Kerry and that little starlet last year," she said, using the handkerchief once again. "And, well, it's my opinion that you did clever job." She moved her cup a few inches forward across the tabletop, watching it. "All right, I suppose I'm still not all that fond of either one of you. But . . . well, okay. Maybe you don't know this, but I don't have a heck of a lot of friends. And nobody I can trust or confide in. Not even my father. I don't imagine you much like me either, but I really need your help."

"We'll help you, Pollyanna," Groucho promised. "Frank, am I speaking for you?"

"Sure, I think it'd be a good idea to help Frances London."

"And me, too?" asked Polly.

After a few seconds I answered, "And you, too, sure, Polly."

"One of the more fascinating aspects of this case is the participation of our old chum, Sergeant Branner of the Bayside constabulary," said Groucho after puffing on his cigar. "I thought we'd be able to dump that lad into the hoosegow for his part in what happened to Peg McMorrow."

"He's slicker than we figured."

"Let's make sure we net him for good this time," he said. "Yes, Rollo, I think we'd best find out who really knocked off this chin-lifter and thereby throw a spanner in the works for Branner. Of course, before we do that we'll have to stop by the public library and find out what a spanner is."

"You mean you will help?" asked the girl, sitting up and smiling at him.

"You have the word of Groucho Marx, for whatever that's worth," he told her. "The last quote I saw was twenty-three dollars and fifty-seven cents, but we're expecting a rally."

"Thank you." Polly caught him by the shoulders and kissed him on the cheek.

"That'll be enough of that." He extricated himself from her grateful grip and stood up. "When we solve this mess, we'll pass the hat, but until then no more smooching, my child."

She said, "You know, Mr. Marx, I just realized you're no-where near as nasty as you pretend to be."

Groucho gasped, took a step to the rear, and slapped the back of his hand to his forehead. "Lord, this innocent waif has found out one of my deepest, darkest secrets," he lamented sadly. "Let's just hope she never learns that the source of all my strength is in my hair."

▌hung around Groucho's kitchen after Polly had been driven off into the night in her limousine. "I still don't quite understand your change of heart about her," I told him. "Only yesterday you were saying that spending time with Polly Pilgrim was like sitting through a plague of locust twice."

He was crouched in front of the open refrigerator, surveying the contents. "Goodness, did I say something that clever, witty, and downright cute?" he asked, registering surprise. "Remind me to contact Bartlett first thing in the morning and urge him to add that to his next compilation of brilliant quotations." Extracting a small casserole dish, he nudged the door shut with his hip. "I'm tempted to add that Bartlett and I make quite a pair, but will probably refrain."

"Wise course," I agreed. "What about your policy shift regarding our resident nightingale?"

Groucho had the dish up close to his face and was scowling into it. "What do you suppose this stuff is?" he wondered. "I'd tag it the remnants of a meatloaf if it weren't for the coconut on top."

"Now I know how Jane feels when she tries to—"

"Gracious me, I should certainly hope you know how that attractive wench feels by now, since you've probably felt her person innumerable times."

"Feels when she tries to get a straight answer out of me."

After sniffing at the dish, he said, "I'm going to chance eating this, whatever it may be." He carried it over to the table and sat across from me. "Very well, Mr. Kaltenborn, I'll come clean."

"Do, yes."

"You'll have to swear, Rollo, not to reveal what I'm about to confide in you to a living soul, nor to any of my assorted brothers."

"Agreed."

"It's common knowledge, by the bye, that the Marx Brothers are also to be found in five flavorful flavors. Especially my brother Pistachio Marx."

"Polly," I reminded.

"Poor Polly isn't an especially likable tyke." He lurched free of his chair and trotted over to the silverware drawer. "And when she materialized on my doorstep this evening, my initial impulse was to apply what Emily Post refers to as the old heave-ho." He returned clutching both a spoon and a fork. "But then she started crying and asked me to help her."

I eyed him. "I've never suspected you of having a sentimental side."

"It was a distinct surprise to me, too," he admitted. "I conclude, however, that because I have a daughter of my own some of my paternal feelings for Miriam must've spilled over onto this midget Lizzie Borden."

"Sounds logical."

"It does?" He shrugged his left shoulder. "Wellsir, there's another first for me."

I picked up my coffee cup and took a sip. "How do you want to start looking into this mess?"

Groucho leaned back in his chair. "I used to know Frances London pretty well—in a strictly avuncular way, you understand," he said. "She was at Paramount the same time we were. I'll fix it so I can visit her in the pokey tomorrow first thing."

"Okay, I'll contact somebody with the Bayside cops and get as much background on the Benninger murder as I can."

"As I recall, not even counting dear Sergeant Branner, the bobbies over there aren't especially given to cooperating with our firm, Rollo."

"True, but I still know a few cops who should help out," I assured him. "I'll also check with a friend or two on the *Times* for background information on both Frances London and Dr. Benninger."

"What time do I have to show up for the broadcast tomorrow?"

"No later than five."

He rubbed his palms together. "Splendid, that means I'll have the whole blessed day to poke my snoot into other people's business." He scooped up a spoonful of the contents of the casserole dish and held it out to me. "Care to share this?"

"Have you decided what the hell it is?"

"No," he said, "which is why I'm looking for volunteers."

Four

The next morning, he told me later, Groucho drove himself to Bayside and parked about a block from the city jail. That's where Frances London had been moved while she was waiting for her hearing.

The day was a gray, foggy one and as he went slouching past a small grocery store, the screen door flapped open, and a husky woman in a polkadot housedress came charging out in his direction.

"Groucho Marx," she cried.

He halted, making a hushing motion. "There's an ordinance against shouting things like that on a public street, madam."

From her purse she yanked out a red-covered autograph book. "Could you say something to my mother?" she asked, thrusting the book and a fat fountain pen toward him.

"Certainly, drag the old girl around to my place any time after nine and I'll recite 'Casey at the Bat' to her."

The woman shuffled closer to him. "No, I mean say something in this autograph album," she explained. "She's a devoted fan of you and your wonderful brothers. So could you write— 'Hi, Helen, I'm Groucho Marx?' "

He accepted the book and pen. "Are you sure that's right?" he asked her, brows furrowing. "I was under the distinct impression that *she* was Groucho Marx and *I* was Helen Twelvetrees."

"No, no, my mother's name is Helen *Kammerman*," she told him. "And you can't possibly be Helen Twelvetrees."

"Well, of course," he said, grinning sheepishly. "I just remembered that ever since that last bout of slippery elm disease I've been Helen Tentrees." He scribbled his signature in the book. "But, say, Helen Tentrees makes a nice moniker. Of course, when Christmas rolls around I use my Santa Monica." He returned everything to the woman and continued on his way.

Frances London sat with her hands folded in her lap. She'd faded quite a bit since Groucho had seen her last. She was thinner, her blond hair no longer had that platinum sparkle and there didn't seem to be any feistiness left in her.

The visiting room at the city jail was a small shadowy place with a wire-mesh screen dividing it in two. It had a sour, forlorn smell. The actress sat in the middle chair of the five straight-back wooden chairs and Groucho sat on the other side of the barrier. There were no other prisoners or visitors there, but in a corner on Frances's side stood a husky police matron with her arms folded.

"Mussolini in drag," murmured Groucho.

"I appreciate your coming to visit, Groucho," Frances said quietly. "Though I'm not sure why you have."

"Polly asked me to, for one thing," he replied, resting his hands on the long, rough wood table he was sitting at. "And I've always had a great deal of admiration for you, especially back in the days when we were organizing the Guild."

Her smile was thin and fleeting. "Long time ago," she said.

"I don't think you know Frank Denby, but he's the boy wonder who's writing the scripts for my radio show," continued Groucho. "Last fall he and I had some luck finding out who killed Peg McMorrow."

"I knew Peg. Poor kid."

Groucho reached into his jacket pocket for a fresh cigar, then remembered he wasn't supposed to smoke here. "Your daughter came to see me last night, Frances," he told her. "She asked Frank and me if we'd help you. We said we would—if you don't mind."

"You mean you want to try to find out who really killed Russ Benninger?"

Groucho nodded. "We're amateurs, but we work pretty well together."

"Yes, you really took care of those bastards who killed Peg," the blond actress said. "I don't know if you or anyone can help me much, Groucho, but I don't see how you can do me any harm and it would be swell to have you on my side."

"Consider us on your side, my dear."

"Roger's provided a lawyer for me."

"I know, yes, that schmuck Caldwell."

"I imagine my former husband believes I really did shoot Russ Benninger while I was in some sort of drunken frenzy," she said. "But Caldwell wants me to plead temporary insanity."

"Yeah, Polly told us."

"Maybe I should go ahead and do that, make it easy for everybody." She raised her head to look directly at him. Her eyes were underscored with darkness. "But, I swear to God, I didn't kill him, Groucho."

31

"No, I don't think you did," he answered. "Not just because I'd like to believe in you—but because I don't see how any woman as bright as you are, kiddo, could cook up such a dumb alibi."

"I've done a lot of dumb things since you knew me last," she admitted. "But this isn't one of them."

"Fill me in," he requested, leaning forward and resting his elbows on the worn table, "on what happened."

"Tuesday afternoon I got a phone call from Nate Winston, my present agent," she began. "Well, it turned out it really wasn't him, but I thought it was. He told me that—"

"Wait, hold it," requested Groucho, holding up his hand. "Nate, as I understand it, denies he phoned you. That gives us two possibilities. He's lying, which wouldn't be an unusual pastime for an agent, or somebody impersonated the guy." The furrows on his brow increased. "Which do you think it was?"

She sighed quietly. "At the time it sounded like Nate," she answered. "But the police questioned him, so did Caldwell. Nate was having a late lunch meeting with a director out at Republic at the time I got the call."

"Still something to look into, though."

"This person, whoever the hell it really was, said that Lou Hagenaur was looking for my type of blonde—or at least the type I used to be—to star in a series of quickie mysteries for the Wheelan Studios," she went on. "Wisecracking blond reporter stuff—if you can't get Glenda Farrell, get Frances London sort of part. I used to know Lou when he was with Fox and I liked him. So it didn't seem funny that he'd want me to drop by his home in Pasadena that night at seven o'clock to talk about the possibility of my doing his series."

"You already have a series in the works at MGM. So why

were you interested in this deal?"

"No, Groucho, all I actually have—or had—with Metro was a one-picture deal. If they liked me in that and if the movie did okay at the box office, then we were going to talk long-term deal," she explained. "Right now, hell, I'd try out for a job as Gene Autry's sidekick if it sounded steady."

"I might take a crack at that one myself. I have quite a reputation as a yodeler, you know," he said. "What transpired once you got to Pasadena? I take it the house wasn't really Hagenauer's?"

"No, it *was* his place," she said. "But he's away at Palm Springs for the whole week."

"Meaning whoever lured you there knew something about Hagenaur's comings and goings."

"I suppose it does, yes. The police, though, think *I* keep up with Lou's schedule and that's why I picked his empty house to use in my fake alibi."

"Who let you into the joint?"

She answered, "When I got to his front door, there was a memo sheet thumbtacked to it. It said—'Back soon, hon. Let yourself in and wait in the living room. Hugs, Lou.'"

"Did he favor expressions like hon and hugs?"

"Used them all the time," Frances said. "Well, I opened the door and walked on in. That was it, Groucho. I wasn't more than a few steps into the hallway when I got sapped."

"Were there lights on in the place?"

"The hall was dark, that's why I didn't notice anybody waiting there to hit me," she said. "But while I was standing out on the porch, I noticed lights in the what must've been the living room. But all the doors opening onto the hallway were closed and hardly any light spilled out."

33

"You didn't see who conked you?"

"No."

"Didn't hear anything, smell anything?"

She frowned and rubbed her fingertip across the bridge of her nose. "That's odd—why'd you mention smell?"

"Oh, it's just something we private eyes inquire about."

"I'd forgotten this, Groucho, but I think I got a whiff of that stuff people use to hide liquor on their breath. A violets sort of scent—Sen-Sen."

"Unfortunately there are quite a few people in Hollywood with bad breath, but it's something."

Frances went on. "After I was knocked out they must've shot me up with something to make me sleep." She pushed up the coarse sleeve of her gray jailhouse dress. There was a small inflamed circle just below her elbow bend. "When I woke up, it was like coming out of ether after an operation. I found myself sprawled on my rug like a drunk and the damned cops were all over the place."

"Did they find any trace of a drug in your blood?"

"They say no. Only too much booze."

Groucho steepled his fingertips under his chin. "What about Dr. Benninger—did you actually threaten the guy?"

"They claim they have witnesses who heard me do that." She shook her head. "But, no, I never did. I was at the Trocadero having a late snack and Russ happened to drop in. He was drunk, which he often was lately. Anyway, he stopped by my table and made some nasty remarks. My escort suggested that he get the hell out of there and the two of them traded a few punches. The only thing I told him was to leave me alone."

"Who was your escort?"

"Not important."

"Even so."

She glanced away. "Jake Hannigan, runs the bookshop on Little Santa Monica," she said finally. "He's married, but not living with his wife."

"I know Jake, he's not a bad chap," said Groucho. "Why'd you and the doc call it quits, child?"

"I realized I didn't much like him."

"Other dames?"

"Sure, there always were," Frances replied, "But the major reason was something else."

"Such as?"

"Well, a couple of times he insisted we have dinner with—"

"Times up, folks." The husky matron had started lumbering over toward them.

"Grant us a few more minutes," requested Groucho.

"Can't. I've already let you run way over, Mr. Marx," she said in her rumbling voice. "The reason for that is that I just loved you in *A Day at the Races*."

He leaned closer to the screen. "Finish up what you were telling me, Frances."

"Go talk to Alice Wakeman. She used to be his nurse and I talked this all over with her. She's a friend of mine, lives in Hollywood."

"Get moving, Mr. Marx." The matron put her big hand on Frances's shoulder, urging her to leave the chair. "Oh, and say hello to the cute Marx Brother for me."

He rose up. "*I'm* the cute Marx Brother, madam."

"No, you're not. I mean the really cute one with the curly hair and the harp. Harpo, that's it. Say hello to him."

He touched the fingertips of his right hand to the partition. "I'll come see you again soon, Frances."

"Thanks, Groucho."

The matron led her out of the room.

Five

When Groucho got back to where he'd parked his Cadillac, there was a tall, thin man in a rumpled blue suit and aging gray fedora leaning against the driver's side door smoking a Camel cigarette.

Groucho halted a few feet from him. "I thought they'd demoted you to walking a beat somewhere in the vicinity of a nice stretch of quicksand, Branner."

"Nope, no such luck, Julius." The lean police sergeant straightened up, grinning, smoke spilling out the corners of his mouth. "Despite all the lousy stories you and your pal, Frankie Denby, spread about me, I'm still on the job. This isn't Hollywood, see, and we don't buy bullshit quite so easy."

Groucho nodded back in the direction of the city jail. "Nevertheless, there are several cells yonder that you'd fit in nicely, sarge," he mentioned. "Were I you, I'd make my reservations plenty of time ahead."

"And you might start thinking of optioning a slab, Julius."

Groucho's cigar had gone dead, and he tugged out a book of Musso and Frank matches and relit it. "Even though I haven't heard chitchat this sparkling since the last time Oscar Levant was on *Information, Please,* I really must be going," he told the policeman as he unlocked his door.

Sergeant Branner patted the hood of the Cadillac and then stepped back and away. "Funny how so many of your tribe go in for big flashy autos."

"Not my tribe, officer. We travel chiefly by pinto pony and sometimes buffalo." Opening the car door, he slid in behind the wheel.

The cop moved closer. "Oh, one more thing," he said, lighting a fresh cigarette from the dying one. "It's not a very smart idea to get yourself involved with the Dr. Benninger business."

"Oh, so?"

"Few years ago when Frances London would get herself into trouble here in Bayside, Paramount would pull strings to get her off and keep her out of the can," said Branner, resting one thin hand on the edge of the open car door. "This time she doesn't have a powerful studio behind her anymore, so that platinum bitch isn't going to get off. I'd be damned unhappy with anybody who tired to see that she did."

After scanning the policeman's gaunt face, Groucho asked, "What the hell are you covering up this time, Branner?"

Branner gave him another thin grin. "Just making conversation, Julius," he maintained. "But it would be a good idea for you to keep in mind that Bayside isn't Beverly Hills and you're not quite so important here as you are there."

"Gracious me, that's distressing news," said Groucho, eyebrows climbing. "Because in Beverly Hills the denizens hold me in low esteem and make it a habit to cast stones at me every time I go driving by. And they do that even though I always cordially inquire, 'Denizen anyone?' "

Branner flicked his cigarette butt in the direction of the Cadillac's fender. "Good-bye, Julius." He turned and went walking away.

Groucho sighed out a breath and started the car. "I don't think," he observed, "that Bayside is going to be a very good market for that gross of welcome mats I've been trying to unload."

While Groucho was visiting the jailhouse, I dropped in at the Bayside Diner where I was going to meet one of my few friends on the Bayside police force. For some reason several seagulls were congregated out in front of the narrow little seafront restaurant.

"Not casting any bird parts today, fellas," I told them as I approached the door. "Sorry."

Giving out annoyed squawks they went scattering away into the gray morning.

Enery McBride was on duty behind the counter. "What do you think?" he asked, turning away from the grill and spreading his arms wide.

"About what? New apron?"

"No, Frank," he said. "My weight, I mean."

Tilting my head, I scrutinized the big husky actor. "Am I obliged to say you look thinner?"

"No, fatter," answered Enery. "I'm in the running for a good part in *Mr. Woo's Murder Cruise* over at Paragon."

"Hey, congratulations. But why do you have to put on weight?"

"I'm being considered for the part of Mr. Woo's new chauffeur." He returned his attention to the flapjacks that were sizzling on the grill. "It's going to be a great dramatic challenge. I not only get to roll my eyes, but I'll be delivering classic lines like, 'I thinks dis ol' house got hants in it, Mr. Woo.' Plus, my favorite of all time, " 'Feets do your stuff.' "

"Still sounds like a step up from 'Carry your bags, sir?' " I sat on a stool after glancing around the small diner. Nobody else at the counter and only one of the booths was occupied, by two blondes drinking coffee and reading the Hollywood trade papers. The cop I was here to meet hadn't arrived yet. "When'll you know for sure?"

"Going in for the final interview the day after tomorrow."

"What's the name of your character?"

"He doesn't have a name, only a nickname."

"Which is?"

"Slow Motion."

"That's worthy of Ben Jonson."

Enery tossed the flapjacks onto a plate. "Describes my personality aptly, yeah," he agreed. "Although I'm more partial to nicknames with an ironic twist, like Snowflake or Sunshine."

"When you're at Paragon, you might ask to try out for the job of Brian Montaine's replacement in *The Legend of King Arthur.*"

"Right, that's a great idea. I can suggest they revise their script so it's more like *The Emperor Jones.*" He poured corn syrup over the hotcakes. "You meeting somebody?"

"Ira Lefcowitz."

"Cop," he said. "Getting back in the detective trade, Frank?"

"Me and Groucho, yeah."

He frowned. "Are you looking into Montaine's death?"

"Nope, no." I stirred two spoons of sugar into my coffee. "Is there anything there to look into?"

He shrugged. "Lady friend of mine works for one of the studio physicians at Paragon." He settled into the chair he kept behind the counter and started in on his breakfast. "Only thing is, she told me that Brian Montaine just had a complete physical exam not more than three four weeks ago. Wasn't a damn thing wrong with his heart then."

"So what killed him?"

"Maybe his habits."

"Which ones?"

Enery pushed the flat of his thumb against his nostril and made a sniffing noise. "That one maybe."

"I hadn't heard that about Montaine."

Enery smiled. "When you're a star, they got publicity people who circulate all sorts of bullshit about you. But they got other publicity people who make damn sure certain kinds of truth never get out. Well, hell, you already know that."

I drank some of my coffee. "What we're looking into is this mess Frances London just got herself into."

"Latest mess in a long series of messes," he said, chewing. "She's got a real knack for getting in trouble. Used to be a pretty good actress though." He glanced over my shoulder as the door opened.

Detective Lefcowitz came in out of the morning, carrying a paper shopping bag. "Morning, one and all. How's the cinema career going, Enery?"

"My rise is about to turn meteoric, Detective."

When he said *Detective,* the two girls sat up straighter and then both slid over closer to the wall of their booth.

Nodding at Lefcowitz's bag, I mentioned, "Looks like you brought me a lot of information, Ira."

He was a middle-size man in his late thirties. "Actually, Frank, since I'm doing a favor for you, a big favor I might add," he said, "I'd like you to do a favor for me in return. C'mon, we'll grab a booth and I'll explain."

Six

As Groucho, in his slouching way, was climbing on foot up through a quiet residential district at the lower edge of the Hollywood hills, he became aware that out on the afternoon street a dusty green Pontiac was moving along parallel to him.

Slowing, he stopped and squinted in the direction of the automobile. It stopped, too.

The window on the passenger side started to roll down and he prepared to fling himself behind the protective trunk of a palm tree about five feet uphill from him. After his encounter with Sergeant Branner, he was a little concerned about his continued well-being.

"Yoo hoo," called someone inside the green car, "yoo hoo."

"You're in the wrong place," he said, pointing back toward where he'd parked his Cadillac. "The yodeling auditions are back that way."

A plump gray-haired woman in a print dress worked her way out of the car, a box camera clutched in both hands. "Mr. Marx," she asked, approaching him in a very tentative way, "would you mind if I took a picture with you?"

Groucho leaped over the flower beds that trimmed the slanting sidewalk and perched on the curb. "Certainly not. What picture shall we take?" he inquired. "I've always been partial to *September Morn,* but you can pick whatever masterpiece you want. They tell me that the *Mona Lisa* is much more valuable, even though the dame in that one is fully clothed." He consulted his gold wristwatch. "Ah, but the *Mona Lisa* is all the way over in Paris and I simply have too many chores today to allow us to pop over there and swipe it. I'm afraid we'll have to steal a picture from one of the local—"

"What I meant, Mr. Marx, is would it be all right if my husband snapped a picture of the two of us."

"Didn't he get enough good ones when he caught us together in the Roosevelt Hotel the other night?" He jumped from the curb to the street. "Myself, I just adored the one of your doing the fan dance atop the room service table. It was, I must tell you, the very first time I'd ever seen anyone do a fan dance with an electric fan and it really and truly—"

"Get back into the car, Myra," suggested her husband from the driver's seat. "These movie stars are all alike."

Groucho went loping around the perplexed woman to peer into the car. "You're absolutely correct, sir. You can't possibly guess how many times a day I'm mistaken for Shirley Temple. The correct answer is twenty-six, but don't let on I slipped it to you." He reached in and shook hands with the plump middle-aged man. "You and Tugboat Annie here have brought a little ray of sunshine into a shut-in's life, but I must be going."

"But what about the photo, Mr. Marx?" asked the woman as he started to walk away.

Groucho halted, spun around. "Okay, kiddo," he said. "Get your hubby out here to snap it before the lunacy commission arrives to throw the net over the lot of us."

"I knew you were a nice man after all, Mr. Marx," she said.

"Under the circumstances," he told her, "I'll overlook that insult."

There wasn't anything in the way of a sea view from the Seaview Court Apartments. A dozen cream-colored stucco cottages with red tile roofs framed a neatly kept courtyard that had a fountain at its center and a half dozen thriving orange trees dotting its green lawn.

Groucho paused at the fountain to gaze at the imitation marble cherub who topped it and held a spouting dolphin in an uneasy embrace.

"I wonder when Harry Cohn posed for that?" he asked himself before continuing on his way.

As he walked up the redbrick steps to the door of apartment 11, he noticed that the lace curtains masking the living room window swayed and flickered.

He tapped on the glass panel of the curtained door with his knuckles.

Nothing happened.

Groucho knocked once more.

He was certain that he was still being observed from within.

"Miss Wakeman," he said, leaning close to the door, "I'm trying to help Frances London."

Very faintly a woman's voice asked, "Who are you?"

"Groucho Marx."

"Oh, c'mon, be serious. Besides, Groucho Marx has a big moustache."

"Greasepaint," he informed the door. He removed the cigar from his mouth and sang a few lines of "Hail, Freedonia." "If that doesn't convince, my dear, I'm prepared to show you my telltale birthmark. That, however, will require a certain amount of public nudity."

After about twenty seconds the door opened a few inches and Dr. Benninger's former nurse looked out, carefully, at Groucho. "Okay, I guess you are who you say you are."

"The last time the government meat inspectors were by the house, they conceded the same thing." The door opened a little farther and he eased into Alice Wakeman's living room.

She was a tall young woman, thin, about thirty, wearing jeans, tennis shoes, and a faded UCLA sweatshirt. "Ever since I heard that Dr. Benninger had been killed," she told him, "I've felt very uneasy."

The room was furnished in department store Swedish modern. "Why?" he asked as he sat in a white armchair.

She seated herself on the blond wood chair opposite him. "Would you like a cup of coffee, Mr. Marx?"

"Not especially. Tell me why you're scared."

"Frances didn't have anything to do with killing him, no matter what the police claim," she answered. "That means whoever did it might also be interested in hurting me."

"Who would they be and why harm you?"

She sighed out a slow breath. "I'm not sure anyone will," she explained. "Because I really don't know all that much about what the doctor was up to. I just can't be certain that they know that."

"You knew enough to quit, though?"

"Between what Frances told me," she went on, "and what I'd figured out for myself, I decided it was time to get out of his office."

"What did she tell you, Alice?"

"Don't you know about that?"

"The matron cut off our conversation before Frances got to the details," he replied. "She said you'd be able to fill me in."

"What bothered Frances were the times they went to the Coconut Grove and were joined by Jack Cortez and his girlfriend."

Groucho straightened in his chair. "Cortez is the Chicago hood who came West to work for that labor racketeer Willie Bioff."

"That's him," she confirmed. "But now he's high up in Joe Tartaglia's outfit."

He rested his cigar in a black ashtray. "Tartaglia is supposed to be the goon who controls the drug trade in Greater LA."

"I don't know exactly what was going on, but Dr. Benninger had some kind of dealings with Tartaglia's people."

"That means he was involved in the narcotics business."

"As I say, I quit before I learned too many of the details."

."You don't know if the doctor was selling drugs or just using them?"

"What I suspect, Mr. Marx, is that Jack Cortez was providing drugs for Dr. Benninger to sell to some of his rich patients."

Leaning back in his chair, Groucho frowned. "This opens up all sorts of interesting new motives for killing the fellow."

"It does," the nurse agreed, "and a lover's quarrel sure as hell isn't one of them."

Seven

I picked up Jane at her boss Rod Tommerlin's self-consciously modern glass-and-redwood house on Palm Lane at a few minutes after one-thirty that afternoon. When I parked at the curb, my car radio was playing Chick Webb's "A-Tisket A-Tasket" and I sat there for about a half minute singing along with Ella Fitzgerald.

The cartoonist's Japanese gardener was trimming the chest-high hedge that paralleled the long, wide driveway. "Very funny," he called to me as I went trotting up the flagstone path toward the house.

Slowing, I inquired, "Which?"

"Your Groucho show last week."

I nodded, grinning, and yelled back, "Wait'll you hear tonight's broadcast."

The front door opened and Jane, a green cardigan over her left arm, stepped out into the afternoon. "I believe," she said, "there's an ordinance against outdoor advertising in this part of Bayside." She came walking toward me.

"I was merely responding to one of my many fans."

"Shouting at the top of your voice constitutes disturbing the peace." She kissed me on the cheek.

I hugged her. "I'm starting to wonder if I really want to cohabit with a woman who frowns on my publicizing my dramatic works."

"Better make up your mind quick, since we're supposed to meet Mr. Farris at a possible house over on Mattilda Road in about twenty minutes." She took my hand and we walked over to my Plymouth coupé.

"Mattilda Road? Do we want to live in a place that's on a street with a godawful name like that?"

"If the rent is right, sure we do."

I held the door open for her and she slid into the passenger seat. I realized that I still liked to watch her long slim legs while she did that.

"Cad," I told myself as I circled the car and climbed in behind the steering wheel.

"How's that?"

"Just reminding myself how far I've sunk since my Boy Scout days." I started the car.

Jane leaned back. "While I think of it," she said, "I've got to attend a funeral tomorrow."

"Oh, whose?"

"Brain Montaine."

I guided my car into Tommerlin's driveway, backed out, and turned around. "I didn't realize you knew him."

"I don't exactly, but his wife and I were sort of friends. She telephoned this morning to ask me to show up and, even though I'm not especially fond of funerals, I agreed."

"Wasn't Montaine divorced?"

"They're only separated," answered Jane. "Dianne Sayler and I went to art school together and were chums back then."

"She's an artist?"

"Yes, and a pretty successful one. She does illustrations for slick magazines like *Collier's,*" she told me. "Every once in a while, when she was still living with Montaine, Dianne'd call and we'd meet for lunch at some extremely fashionable bistro on or near Rodeo Drive. She's not a bad person, although she tends to complain a heck of a lot about most everything."

"Do you want me to tag along?"

"Nope, I'll solo on this." She shook her head. "Besides you're going to be doubly busy now that you and Groucho have hung out your shingle again."

I tugged at my earlobe. "Am I sensing a snide tone creeping into your voice, my dear?"

Smiling, she spread her hands wide. "Hey, I'm all for your helping Frances London," Jane assured me. "She hasn't had an especially happy life and right now she needs all the help she can get. Besides, I know that you and Groucho are very effective at this sort of thing."

I turned right on Westwind Road. "I'm beginning to think she probably is innocent."

"What did Detective Lefcowitz tell you this morning?"

I sighed. "Well, unfortunately, the first thing Ira told me is that he wants to be a writer."

"A radio writer, you mean?"

"No, a pulp magazine writer. He discovered *Black Mask* and *Dime Detective* couple years back," I said. "What he's done is turn out a story—a very long story—about a Hollywood private eye."

"A private eye like J. Hawkshaw Transom."

"Not exactly, no. This is a very tough, deadly serious operative christened Slug Farrell."

Jane grinned. "That's a nifty name. Yes, I think I could place my faith in a man named Slug. It suggests strength and dependability and isn't a wishy-washy name like, oh, say, Frank."

"Then perhaps you'd like to read through a twenty-five-thousand-word Slug Farrell yarn entitled *Dames Love Diamonds* and critique the damn thing."

"Do you absolutely have to?"

"Pretty sure I do if I want to continue to have this particular cop's cooperation."

She asked, "So what about the murder of this plastic surgeon?"

"Well, there are several things that make me think that Frances London couldn't have had anything to do with the killing of Dr. Benninger." I spotted Mattilda Road coming up on my right. "What number?"

"Eleven-forty."

"Then we want to turn left."

Jane said, "What things?"

"For one, the doctor was shot in the back of the head at very close range," I replied, tapping the back of my head with a forefinger. "That was done while the guy was facedown on his living room carpet."

"What's the police theory? That she knocked him down somehow and then sat on his back while she shot him?"

"They simply say she did it, especially our favorite cop, Sergeant Branner," I said. "But, after getting a look at the photos of the scene and reading over the autopsy report, I'd guess this was more in the line of an execution."

"You mean as in a gangster killing?"

"Right, or some kind of revenge thing," I said. "I can't see how a hundred-twenty-pound woman could knock off a six foot tall two-hundred-pound guy that way."

"She could've got him drunk first."

I gave a negative shake of my head. "No evidence of alcohol or drugs in his blood," I said. "And no sign that Dr. Benninger was slugged beforehand."

"Your detective friend pass along anything else?"

"They got on to Frances because of a telephone tip," I added. "From the ever popular anonymous."

"The question being—how did that person know that there'd been a murder?"

"Exactly, yeah." I sighted the house on the right. Easy to do, since there was a large multicolored Sunnyland Realtors for rent sign planted on the large green front lawn. "Meaning anon. is the true culprit."

At least half again as large as either of our cottages, it was a Spanish-style one-story house, cream stucco and red tile roof. There were well-kept shrubs and neat flower beds and the whole place looked well taken care of.

"Think this will make a suitable love nest?" I asked while getting out of the car.

"Let's go find out," she said.

Eight

The day had brightened somewhat and by the time Groucho was loping along Little Santa Monica Boulevard toward Hannigan's Bookstore a hazy yellow sun was visible in the afternoon sky. The shop sat between a French restaurant that had been in operation a little over three weeks and a store that specialized in what appeared to be authentic Swedish Modern furniture. A pyramid made up of about thirty copies of *The Yearling* dominated the small display window and rising up only half as high was a stack of *Homage to Catalonia.*

"I thought Catalonia was something they served in Italian restaurants," mumbled Groucho as he reached for the highly polished brass knob on the dark wood door.

The door opened before he touched it and Nathanael West stepped out onto the sidewalk, a parcel of books tucked under his arm. He was a thin, pale man in his middle thirties, wearing tweedy clothes and a tan snapbrim hat. "Oh, hi, Groucho," he said, smiling.

"Nathan, if I am ever forced to grow a real moustache, I intend to model it after yours." He shook hands with the writer. "To paraphrase Disraeli, how's tricks?"

West shrugged. "I'm still working on the novel about Hollywood," he answered. "And making a living writing a lousy script for RKO."

"There's a coincidence for you. My siblings and I are preparing to star in a lousy script at RKO."

"They have more than one of those over there."

Groucho reached again for the doorknob. "Give my best to Sid and Laura," he said. "I envy your being related to such a literary luminary as Sid Perelman, an author I rank right up there with Edgar Rice Burroughs, Bertha M. Clay, and the fellow who writes all those Burma Shave signs."

"Next time I see them, I'll suggest that he adopt you."

"No need, since I intend to leave myself on his doorstep in a wicker basket. The only thing that's holding me back is finding a basket of sufficient capacity."

West said, "Let me ask you something."

"This doesn't involve naming any of the capitals of states, does it?"

West made a vague gesture toward the street. "You've been out here longer than I have," he said. "Don't you ever get tired of all the shit in Hollywood."

"Not thus far," replied Groucho. "And that is chiefly because we're still busy mining it for gold."

West shrugged again. "Well, it's my theory the whole place is going to burn down eventually, so it really doesn't matter." He tapped Groucho on the arm and went walking away.

Groucho eased into the bookshop.

It was long, narrow, and shadowy, its tables and shelves offering a mix of popular fiction and political works.

A thin young woman in a very large gray cardigan sweater approached him. "Might I help you, sir?"

"I hope so, miss," he said. "I'm frightfully eager to read that novel about a lad who raises a lovable deer. Afraid, though, that I can't dredge up the title."

Her nose wrinkled as she nodded toward the front window. "Oh, that'd be *The Yearling.* Everybody is reading that stupid book."

Groucho frowned. "That's not the one I'm seeking, my dear. The novel I want is about a little nipper who raises a stray deer in his Moroccan-style mansion in Bel Air. Then, after he teaches it to do tricks, tap-dance, and imitate Jimmy Cagney, he stars it in a series of boffo B-movies about Rex the Wonder Buck. I think it was written by André Gide."

The thin girl's shoulders rose and fell as she realized, "Oh, you're Groucho Marx." She didn't sound especially enthusiastic about her discovery.

"You've penetrated my disguise," he acknowledged. "Is Jake Hannigan around and about?"

She pointed toward the rear of the store. "You'll find him back in his office," she said, watching Groucho with her head slightly tilted to the left. "What sort of books do you really like to read, Mr. Marx?"

"At the moment I'm working my way through *Tarzan and the Lost Delicatessen,*" he answered. "Once I finish that, I'm hoping to dip into Burton's *Anatomy of Melancholy* and then the sequel, *Anatomy of Melancholy Baby.*"

"Maybe you ought to browse through our psychiatry section before you see Mr. Hannigan," she suggested on leaving him.

Jake Hannigan was a handsome man of forty-one with a deep outdoor tan and wavy dark hair. The fact that he was only five foot one was what prompted him to give up his movie ambitions and open a bookstore some nine years earlier.

He was sitting in a large armchair in the small, cluttered back office of his shop, drinking tomato soup out of a cracked coffee mug. "We're having a special meeting of the Anti-Nazi League at Eddie Robinson's place tonight, Groucho," he said. "Can you make it?"

Groucho shook his head, lifted a tied bundle of back issues of *The American Mercury* off a bentwood rocker and seated himself. "I have to do not one but two broadcasts of my radio show tonight, Jake," he explained. "One for the East and one for the West. Thank the lord we don't also have to do separate ones for the North and South."

"Sorry, I forgot all about *Groucho Marx, Master Detective.*"

"We now call it *Groucho Marx, Private Eye.* Are you no longer a devout listener?"

"I've been spending a hell of a lot of nights with meetings and committees," he said. "But I do still drink your coffee."

"We lost our coffee sponsor just before Christmas," Groucho told him. "Fact of the matter is, Santa Claus dropped the cancellation down my chimney on Christmas Eve. One of his reindeer—we've got the suspects narrowed down to Donner, Blitzen, and Trixie—dropped something else but we just left that lying amidst the ashes."

The book dealer said, "We're thinking of putting on a benefit show for the Spanish Loyalists. Can we count on you for that?"

"As long as it's not on a Thursday night," he replied, "and I can sing selections from Gilbert and Sullivan."

Hannigan winced slightly. "Okay, I suppose so," he conceded after sipping his hot soup. "But you'll wear your moustache, won't you? Some people don't recognize you without—"

"That's going to depend upon the outcome of a case before the State Supreme Court right now," said Groucho, running his fingertips over his hairless upper lip. "When we left MGM, Louis B. Mayer claimed that he still owned my moustache and he wouldn't return it. I hear he's been allowing Clark Gable, William Powell, and the gent who makes the chicken soup in the commissary to wear it whenever they please. I'm not even certain, should I win the case, that I want to use that thing again after they've been sticking it—"

"You paint it on with greasepaint," reminded Hannigan.

"Jove, you're right about it's only being the Platonic idea of a moustache. What a silly little fool I've been." Groucho rocked back and forth once in the chair. "Perhaps we can get down to the actual purpose of my visit."

"You're working as an amateur detective again, trying to help Frances London."

Groucho straightened up. "How'd you know that?"

"It was on Johnny Whistler's broadcast this morning."

"I'm definitely going to have to start tuning him in. I'd gotten the impression, considering his voice is so high pitched, that only dogs could hear him. But apparently I was in error."

"Do you think Frances has got a chance?"

"I'm damn sure she didn't kill Dr. Benninger." He took a cigar out of a pocket of his checkered sportcoat. "But faith isn't going to spring Frances—we have to prove who really did knock off the guy."

Hannigan said, "I saw Russ Benninger just last Saturday."

"Where?"

"He came into the shop here."

Groucho's eyebrows rose. "Weren't you sworn enemies after that tussle at the Trocadero?"

"Benninger was a customer of mine for years, Groucho. He was a real California history buff," explained Hannigan. "When he was here Saturday afternoon, he apologized for the business at the Troc, admitted that he was drunk and out of control. Claimed he'd been under a lot of pressure lately and—"

"Pressure from what?"

The book dealer shrugged. "No idea, Groucho," he answered. "He seemed to be in a jittery mood when he was here, but he didn't mention anything about expecting to be shot dead within the next few days."

"Was he by himself?"

"No, Dracula's Daughter was with him."

"You're alluding to Maddy Dubay?"

"The same, a woman who's a walking definition of a shrew." He drank some of his soup. "She's not a bad screen writer. I heard she was doing some last-minute rewrites on *The Legend of King Arthur,* keeping about a day ahead of the shooting. Don't know where that leaves her now that Brian Montaine's kicked off."

"Was Maddy with him that night at the Trocadero?"

"She was, yes."

Groucho said, "Now about what went on. Did Frances threaten to kill Benninger?"

"She didn't, no," he answered. "The Bayside cops claim to have witnesses who'll swear otherwise, but that's a lot of crap. Nobody could've heard anything, because there wasn't a damn thing to hear."

"What did happen?"

"The doctor was drunk—and I think he'd been squabbling with Maddy, too. On his way out he noticed us and came over, staggering plenty, to make some nasty remarks to Frances."

"Such as?"

"Gutter stuff," said Hannigan, frowning. "Accusing her of being a tramp, of getting drunk again. I told him to take a hike and, to back up my suggestion, I stood up and punched him a couple times." He paused, exhaling and then inhaling deeply. "Frances did used to behave in a pretty wild way, sure, but that all ended years ago. She's okay now and I wasn't going to let that bastard talk to her that way." He paused again. "All right, I guess that makes me a hypocrite, continuing to keep him as a customer. But I figure, he apologized and I might as well take his money."

Putting the cigar in his mouth, Groucho leaned back in the rocker. "Any ideas about who might've sent Benninger on to glory?"

"It wasn't Frances," he said. "Oh, and it wasn't me."

"You wouldn't rub out a paying customer."

Hannigan said, "I wish I could tell you who'd make a likely suspect, Groucho. I have heard that he was the kind of doctor who'd do favors for his patients."

"What sort of favors?"

"You know, ranging from setting up an abortion to providing narcotics," he said. "That's only hearsay, though, and I don't have any real information."

"At this stage," said Groucho, "I'm accepting hearsay."

Nine

May Sankowitz' office at *Hollywood Screen Magazine* was at least three times larger than the one she'd occupied at the *Los Angeles Times* when she'd been posing at Dora Dayton and handling the lovelorn column. May herself was a small, slim woman in her late forties and she was currently a honey blonde.

From the high, wide window you could look down on Wilshire Boulevard. There were no framed photos on the eggshell-white walls. But sitting sideways on her desk was a large framed glossy of Abraham Lincoln.

"Congratulations on the new job," I said, sitting down and facing her. "Why Lincoln?"

She sighed. "It isn't Abe Lincoln," she answered, "it's Slim."

"Slim the lengthy cowboy actor?"

"That Slim, yes." May sighed again. "Usually my romantic interludes with lanky dimwits only last a matter of weeks. For some reason, though, I'm still entangled with Slim."

"Love, do you think?"

"Search me." She shrugged and spread her hands wide. "If I were still batting out Dora's gush, I might be able to advise myself about my dilemma. But as a purveyor of movieland gossip,

I haven't got the faintest notion of why I continue to see the guy."

I pointed a thumb at the picture. "So why's he got up as Lincoln?"

"Slim is playing Honest Abe in a movie. Well, not a movie really, a serial," she explained. "Over at Columbia, a twelve-chapter epic called *The Phantom of Gettysburg*. Dick Foran is starring, along with Fuzzy Knight."

"An all-star cast," I observed. "As I was saying on the phone, May, I need some information about—"

"First I'd like some info from you, Frank dear."

"Well, Jane and I are just good friends and rumors of any impending—"

"Would that either you or that terrific girl were of any interest to the vast army of dimwits who read *Hollywood Screen* every month in beauty parlors across the land," said May. "No, what I need to know more about is Polly Pilgrim, that freckle-faced little songbird."

"I can't talk about her mother's case or—"

"No, not the murder. I don't cover crime," cut in May, tapping on her desk with a sharp-pointed yellow pencil. "But I just heard that your dumpy little darling is about to sign a very big contract with Paragon Pictures. The Zansky Brothers, who run that joint and are still in mourning for the late Brian Montaine, are betting she's going to be another Deanna Durbin."

"So does our sponsor, Colonel Mullen. But then, he also believes his puddings are edible," I said. "If you're asking me to confirm the rumors, May, I'm afraid I can't."

"Can't or won't?" She tapped again with the pencil.

"I haven't heard a damn thing about any lucrative new movie contract for the kid. Really and truly."

"I suppose you'd cross your heart and hope to die if I so requested?"

"I'd even swear on the Bible, if you had such a thing in your office."

She made a brief low humming sound. "Doesn't that moppet confide in you guys? I mean, now that you and Groucho are doing your Sherlock and Watson act for her benefit."

"Polly talks about her mother's problems when we get together, May," I said. "Not her own career."

"Although I've always been petite and adorable myself, I can sympathize with that kid," she said. "She's got a terrific voice, but pretty she isn't. Going to make it tough for her to compete with a cutie pie like Deanna Durbin or even Judy Garland."

"It's just a phase."

"Ugly's not a phase, sweetheart."

"Can we chat about Dr. Benninger and Frances London now?"

"Next time you bump into Little Miss Melody, can you, sort of subtly, inquire about the Paragon deal?"

"Surely you've got better sources of information than me," I said. "But, yeah, I can give it a try."

"Despite your lack of celebrity, Frank, you're a movieland insider now. Hobnobbing with Groucho Marx, scripting a hit radio show, solving baffling Hollywood mysteries."

"Dr. Benninger," I reminded.

May scowled at Slim's Lincoln portrait, then reached out and turned it facedown. "Most of what I know about that prominent plastic surgeon I couldn't run in my gossip column here at the magazine," she began. "But the gent did a lot more than streamline aging and inadequate pusses."

"For example?"

"The word was that if you needed dope to perk you up, help you snooze of an evening, or just make you feel that life wasn't as shitty as it was looking—well, hey, kindly old Doc Benninger was the medic for you."

I asked, "Where was he getting his drugs?"

"Not too tough for a doctor to get morphine and stuff like that," May answered. "For the more exotic products—like heroin and coke—he apparently had some good Combination sources."

"Joe Tartaglia?"

"None other, so I heard," she said, nodding. "Plus Tartaglia's little helper, Jack Cortez." Pausing, she looked directly across her desk at me. "I know you ran up against some of our eminent local hoodlums while you and Groucho were finding out who killed Peg McMorrow—but those guys were lambs compared to Tartaglia's bunch. So, Frank dear, you be real careful if you go anywhere near those bastards."

"I was planning to be careful," I assured the columnist. "The way Dr. Benninger was done in—it looks like a mob killing to me."

"It sure could've been, all the more reason to play it very carefully, dear."

"Let's say," I suggested, "that it wasn't about drugs and that Tartaglia's not involved at all. Who else?"

She gave a slight shrug. "Benninger fooled around a good deal. So there're probably a long line of unhappy husbands who might've pumped a few slugs into his lecherous carcass."

"Any names?"

"I'd have to dig some to get you the latest, up-to-date list, Frank."

"Can you?"

"Sure, yeah, especially if you can get me something about that impending deal of little Polly's. Is the kid signing to sing for the Zanskys and for how much?"

I asked, "Is there anything in Frances London's past that might have inspired somebody to knock off the doctor?"

"It wouldn't be jealousy I don't think," she said. "At least that fascist ex-husband of hers, Roger Pilgrim, didn't much care about her anymore. He's only interested in making lucrative deals for Polly." She leaned back in her chair. "I can ask some discreet questions, see if that turns up anything."

I stood up. "I'd appreciate that, May."

"Oh, hey, I just thought of something," she said, rising. "There was a story going around about a year ago, I heard this while I was still with our alma mater, the *Times*. Anyway, Dr. Benninger supposedly, while recovering from a binge, botched up one of his patient's faces pretty badly and left her looking like Boris Karloff on a bad day."

"Who was she?"

May said, "Fading actress named Elena Stanton. Remember her?"

"In some early talkies, yeah. Blonde, on the tall side, faint lisp."

"That's the lady in question."

"Any idea where she is now?"

"None, but I'll find out if you think it's important."

"So far I haven't any damn notion as to what's important and what isn't," I admitted, reaching across and shaking her hand.

"Most people in this phony town kiss me good-bye, you know."

"That's what makes me such a refreshing exception." Grinning, I left her office.

Ten

Polly Pilgrim scowled. "That's *not* why she was seeing that awful doctor. It wasn't to get dope."

I said, "That's not what we're suggesting."

Groucho inquired, "Child, have you ever heard of Sarah Bernhardt, also known as the Divine Sarah?"

"No, never."

"Well, Sarah Bernhardt was considered just about the finest stage actress of her day, perhaps of all time," he explained. "Her only flaw was that she had a wooden leg. Do you have any notion how she came to lose her leg?"

"I don't, no."

"It was because she interrupted once too often whilst I was having a conversation with a colleague." He reached across the restaurant booth table to pat her on the head.

"Ouch," she remarked.

"What Groucho is suggesting," I told her, "is that you let us go on comparing notes with fewer intrusions."

"Exactly my point, Rollo." He was sitting across the table from the singer and me, a steno notebook open beside his plate of cheese blintzes.

After our 6:00 P.M. broadcast of *Groucho Marx, Private Eye* we'd walked two blocks to Moonbaum's Hollywood Delicatessen. Polly had insisted on tagging along and Groucho, after producing an impressive range of groans and pained expressions, had agreed.

"I'm," she reminded him now, "your client. I've got a right to say things sometimes."

"Clients should be seen and not heard."

"That's *children* who should be seen and not heard."

"You still qualify, Pollyanna." He took a few more bites of his blintz before picking up his Waterman fountain pen. "What we have to establish, Frank, is whether or not Benninger was involved in some aspect of the drug business. And if his untimely demise is tied in with that unsavory sideline of his."

"I've got at least one informant who can get me something about that." I drank some of my coffee. "I don't think we want to contact Tartaglia or Cortez directly."

"No, and we don't want to drive up to Frisco and jump off the recently completed Bay Bridge." He smiled at Polly. "That's how we gumshoes stay alive, my child, by avoiding unnecessary risks."

"I'll also look into the possibility that Dr. Benninger has some disgruntled former patients who might want to get revenge on him."

"First thing in the morning," said Groucho, "I'll leap from my trundle bed, whatever that is, and track down the incomparable Maddy Dubay. As quite probably the most recent intimate chum of the doc's, she may have something to contribute to our fund of information."

Polly asked quietly, "What about this Sergeant Branner that you mentioned, Mr. Marx? Why did he bother to warn you off?"

Groucho held up his forefinger. "A wise and insightful query, Little Dorrit," he said. "Can you get back to Detective Lefcowitz, Frank, and find out what Branner's angle is?"

"I was figuring to do that, Groucho, yes."

"They're having my mother's hearing tomorrow morning," said Polly. "If they'll allow bail, she could get out of that terrible place."

"I imagine Caldwell can arrange that," Groucho told the girl. "Is your father prepared to take care of the bail bond?"

Polly nodded. "He told me he's going to spare no expense," she answered. "I'm really hoping that this whole mess will bring them back together again."

Groucho's eyebrows rose. "What would you pick, Frank?" he asked me. "Life in a cell at the Tehachapi prison for ladies or sharing a bed with Roger Pilgrim?"

"That's a tough one, Professor Quiz."

"It is, bless my bones, a near classic example of the old Scylla and Charybdis dilemma," he observed. "Not to mention the equally dangerous Wheeler and Woolsey double bill. Or the— Yoicks!"

Polly had apparently kicked him in the shin.

She settled back, saying, "I'm sorry."

"I've previously looked this up in the *Private Investigator's Manual, Almanac and Perpetual Calendar,* my child," he told her, "and it clearly states therein that clients are forbidden to kick their detectives. The vice versa setup, however, is allowable in most states and territories that—"

"I lost my temper," Polly said. "I apologize."

Groucho stroked his chin, scanned her, and adopted his old vaudeville Dutch accent. "I think we're making progress with this patient, Carl. She actually apologized for a rude—"

71

"That's marvelous, Groucho, really." A broad-shouldered gray-haired man was standing beside our delicatessen booth. He was recently shaven, wearing an expensive double-breasted gray suit and a quiet gray silk tie. "I wish I had the ability to kid with Polly the way you do."

"Buy a copy of my book, *How to Kid Around in Ten Easy Lessons,*" Groucho suggested to Roger Pilgrim.

The political publicist slid in, uninvited, and sat next to Groucho. "You and I are usually on different sides of the fence, and I really think it's a mistake on your part to hang around with radicals like Fredric March and Melvyn Douglas. But, even so, I have a great deal of admiration for you, Groucho, and I'm really pleased that you're helping Polly."

Groucho, lips tight shut, made a low growling sound. Then he said, "Forgive the unseemly noise—I was biting my tongue."

Pilgrim leaned his elbows, carefully, on the tabletop and smiled at his daughter. "They told me at the studio you were over here, princess," he said. "I hope you don't mind my dropping in on you and your friends."

"Is it about my mother?"

Pilgrim stretched, took hold of her hand. "Yes, I do have some news, pet. I had a nice conversation with Mr. Caldwell late this afternoon," he told her. "He assures me that he fully expects to get the judge to agree to bail for your mother. She should be free by midday tomorrow."

"That's wonderful, father." She squeezed his hand, laughing.

"We have to keep in mind, remember, princess, that she's still going to have to stand trial for murder."

"I know, yes, but at least she'll be out of that awful place."

"For a time." He let go of her hand. "Groucho, I'd appreciate it if you'd allow me to offer you a fee for all that you're doing."

"No, sorry." Groucho gave a negative shake of his head. "So far we run our detective business on a completely altruistic basis—somewhat in the manner of Robin Hood. If you can envision a middle-aged Yiddish Robin Hood." He glanced over at me, eyebrows rising. "I suppose Rueben Hood would be too obvious a name?"

"Too obvious for the public in general or too obvious for you to say?"

"Nevermind, let it pass." He gathered up our check and handed it to Polly's father. "Since you're in a generous mood, Pilgrim, you *can* pay this while we pussyfoot back for the repeat broadcast." He stood. "Keep in mind that I've a reputation for being a lavish tipper."

Harry Whitechurch usually had two Manhattans with his dinner, which resulted in his being even more deep-voiced and jovial on our nine o'clock broadcast.

His third commercial was particularly exuberant that evening. "Just taste a succulent serving of Mullens Vanilla Pudding, folks, and you'll know why Mullens is the greatest name in pudding," he concluded. "And, you can take my word for this, folks, every scrumptious spoonful will have you exclaiming, 'My oh my, it's Mullens'—and it's mighty mighty good!' "

Up in the control booth Annie Nicola pointed at her ear, then made a lower-it motion with her hand.

The announcer nodded, grinned up at her, and lowered his voice a few notches. "And now we return to the gloomy Uppercase Mansion for the exciting conclusion of tonight's hilarious episode of *Groucho Marx, Private Eye.*"

I think I should point out that I didn't write the commercials or the segue lines. The colonel's New York advertising agency provided that stuff.

Margaret Dumont, as Mrs. Uppercase, was sharing a microphone with Groucho.

Groucho rested his hand on her backside. "Feast your eyes on this chamois bag, dear lady. Or perhaps you'd rather join me in a chorus of 'I Wish I Could Chamois Like My Sister Kate'?"

She took hold of his coat sleeve between thumb and forefinger and lifted his hand away. "Oh, Mr. Transom, have you found my missing jewel and brought it back to me?"

"I have indeed, old girl. This is the fabulous Keeler Ruby."

"I shall be eternally grateful."

"I don't think I can wait that long," read Groucho. "So here's my bill and my expense account right now, my dear."

Our sound man crumpled a sheet of paper up close to his mike.

Margaret Dumont said, "I'm afraid you're going to have to explain many of these items on your list of expenses."

"I was afraid of that. Okay, fire away."

"What does this mean—overhead?"

"I bought a toupee."

"But, Mr. Transom, you have a perfectly good head of hair."

"This toupee was a birthday present for the dean of my mail-order detective school. Perhaps you've heard of him—Gunga Dean?"

"Now how about this item—two hundred dollars for greasing palms."

"Well, I had to pay out a few bribes."

"Three hundred dollars for greasing pigs?"

"We took some time out for a bit of sport."

"Barn raising?"

74

"That was my fault, Mrs. Uppercase. One of the important clues rolled under the barn and there was nothing to do but lift it up."

"Barn setting?"

"Obviously, we couldn't leave the barn up in the air. I had to pay some roustabouts to set it down again."

"I suspect that this is so much filmflam."

"No, no, the filmflam is listed under Incidentals."

"And how do you explain one hundred dollars for flowers?"

"Those were the roses I showered you with on *your* birthday. I was toying with the idea of giving *you* the toupee but the dean kicked up such a fuss that—"

"You have the audacity to ask me to pay for my own flowers?"

"You wouldn't want some total stranger to get stuck with the tab, would you?"

"I'm very disappointed with you, Mr. Transom."

"Not half as disappointed as you're going to be when you find out that the ruby is actually a glass eye."

After clearing his throat off mike, Harry said, "You've just heard *Groucho Marx, Master Detective.* Brought to you each week at this time by Mullens Pudding—It Comes In Five Flavorful Flavors. Tonight's script was by Frank Denby and our director was Annie Nicola. Tippsy Transom was played by Polly Pilgrim, the little songbird of the cinema. Hans Conreid appeared as Inspector Sprudelwasser, Rob Stolzer was Rosco. Others in the cast were Gale Gordon, Jerry Marcus, and Elena Steier. And now here's an important message from our star, Groucho Marx."

Groucho leaned toward the mike. "Good night, folks."

Annie touched her finger to her nose, smiled, and made a throat cutting motion. "I was quite impressed by your deportment tonight, Grouch," she said over her mike.

"That's because I've taken a part-time job in a deportment store," he explained, taking a cigar out of his coat pocket.

Polly came over and hugged him. "You were even funnier on the second broadcast, Mr. Marx," she told him.

"And you were even more lyrical, dear child."

Harry eyed me. "Is this a mirage?"

"It's a new era of good feelings," I said.

"Won't last," he said and walked off.

Eleven

I didn't say that," said Jane.

"It's okay if you don't think a line is funny," I assured her. "I can detach myself from my scripts. Of course, I have to admit, I thought last night's show was exceptionally funny."

"A laugh riot?"

"Damn close to."

"Um." She was hunched in front of the dressing table mirror, adjusting a small black hat.

"Do you always put the hat on before the dress?"

She was wearing only a lacy black slip. "Hey, do I razz you because you put on your shoes before your trousers?"

It was a rainy Friday morning, windy.

"So tell me which line in last night's show you didn't think was funny."

"*Lines.*"

I'd been leaning in the bedroom doorway. I straightened up. "I thought it was just one."

Jane tilted her head to the left, then the right. "Not somber enough," she decided as she took off the hat.

"Which lines?"

"Well, the stuff about chamois like my Sister Kate was a little too obvious."

"But that's the Groucho Marx style," I explained, patiently I thought. "Every so often we have to pop in an audacious pun or—"

"Audacious is one thing, but dumb is something else again."

I was silent for nearly a minute. "It has long been my custom," I announced finally, "never to debate with a woman who's in her underwear. Far too distracting. Once, while on the debating team in high school, I was quite taken aback when Doris Dinkins appeared at the podium wearing nothing more than—"

"Whoa, stop." She smiled over her bare shoulder at me. "I'm sorry I'm in a bitchy mood. It's probably because I'm not all that fond of funerals."

"So you said. Okay, we'll change the subject," I told her. "What about the new house? Do you really—Not, by the way, that I resent any sort of positive criticism about my writing—do you really like it?"

"I do, absolutely. Don't you? I think we ought to call Mr. Farris this afternoon and tell him we'll definitely take it."

I nodded. "I like it, sure. But maybe we ought to look at a few more before—"

"Keep in mind, Frank, that this is only going to be temporary." She bent, lifted another hat out of the hat box sitting on the rug. "We're on our way toward being immensely rich—you with your eventual movie scripts, me with *Hollywood Molly.* So we have to think of this new place as simply a temporary stopover on the road to fame, fortune, and Beverly Hills. Or Bel Air."

"Actually my ultimate goal in a home has always been a

cottage small by a waterfall, but if you like this new dump—it's okey-doke by me."

"You're one man in a hundred, Frank."

"Which one?"

"Number twenty-six last time we checked." She tried on the new hat, didn't like it, tossed it back in the box. "I just don't seem to have any serious hats."

"Wear a scarf."

"You can't wear a scarf to the Hollywood Memorial Park, it's too ritzy a place. Valentino is buried there after all," she told me, "besides, whenever I wear a scarf I look like Una O'Conner or somebody in a Sean O'Casey play."

"You're cuter. The fact is—"

The phone started ringing out in the living room. "Answer it, will you, Frank?"

I obliged. "Hello?"

"Hi, Frank." It was Enery McBride at the Bayside Diner.

"Did you get the part in the Mr. Woo movie?"

"I did, yeah, but that's not why I'm phoning," he said. "There's somebody here wants to see you."

"Someone who intends me bodily harm perhaps?"

"Nothing like that. It's a cop who says he's a buddy of that other cop, your pal Detective Lefcowitz," Enery explained. "He seems awfully eager to have a conversation with you, but he provided me with no details."

"Okay, tell him I'll be there in about ten minutes."

"Groucho?" asked Jane.

"Nope, it was Enery. Says some cop wants to see me at the café."

She came into the room, a pair of black silk stockings in her hand. "Quite a few of the Bayside force aren't especially fond of you," she reminded me. "Be careful, huh?"

"I was planning to," I said, kissing her. "Have fun at the funeral."

The thin, pale blonde in the black bathing suit told Groucho, "You don't look like much off the screen."

He took a slow puff of his cigar before saying, "If you reflect for a moment, dear lady, you'll come to realize that I don't look like all that much *on* the screen."

"Must you smoke that terrible cigar?"

"I've been experiencing a slight financial recession and terrible cigars are all I can afford."

"Snuff it out in that ashtray."

He ground the cigar butt into the seashell ashtray that rested on a rattan table beside the large indoor swimming pool. "I can't say much for your poolside manner," he mentioned.

"As if I give a shit," said Maddy Dubay. "You're damn lucky I even agreed to waste my time talking to you at a time like this, Groucho."

"Yes, I figured you were in mourning for Russell Benninger soon as I noticed the black swimsuit." He dropped into a deck chair near hers.

Through the glass wall of the indoor pool you could see down across an acre or so of landscaped gardens. There were what were probably abstract metal sculptures, large and painted in bright primary colors, out in the rainy morning. A forlorn seagull was perched on a big yellow rectangle.

"Did you plan to sit there gawking at my LoBruttos or did you have something you wished to talk about with me?"

"You have handsome LoBruttos," conceded Groucho, "but

I was actually looking out at those gaudy hunks of scrap metal somebody dumped on your lawn."

"LoBrutto is a sculptor," Maddy informed him. "Or did you already know that and simply jump at the chance to make a crude double entendre remark?"

"LoBrutto and I took Metal Shop together back at PS Ninety-three," he said. "What do you know about Dr. Benninger's death?"

Her laugh was harsh and nasal. "You're really a dreadful man," she told him, reaching down to pick up her cocktail glass off the turquoise tiles. "It's quite obvious you try to hide your personal inadequacies behind the façade of a cheap wisecracking buffoon."

"That's absolutely true and only today that cheap buffoon told me he's raising the rent that I have to pay on his façade." He took a fresh cigar from the pocket of his greenish sportcoat, studied it and put it away again. "Benninger?"

After finishing off the highball, the screen writer said, "As much as I'd like to see that bitch, Frances London, spend the rest of her miserable life in the hoosegow," she told him, "I don't think she had a damn thing to do with killing poor Russell."

He shifted in his chair, watching her. "Who did?"

"I'd guess probably his hoodlum buddies."

"Are we alluding to Tartaglia and Jack Cortez?"

"Among others, yes. Russell had been a business associate of theirs for . . . well, for far too long."

"If Cortez or one of his goons did do the doctor in," said Groucho, "what was the reason?"

"I'm not at all certain, Groucho." She left her chair and walked slowly around the pale blue pool. At the glass wall she stood looking out into the wet, gray morning. "Bring me my robe."

"Yes, missee." He grabbed it off the chair back, went trotting over to the writer.

"Russell was extremely upset during the last few days of his life." She slipped into the white terry-cloth robe he was holding for her. "Anguished, as though he had some very unpleasant task to face."

"Didn't he confide any details in you?"

"We slept together, but I wasn't his confidant," she said. "Russell never discussed his dealings with Cortez. What I knew about was all that I picked up by paying attention." She turned her back on the view, thrusting her hands deep into the pockets of the robe. "I'm considerably brighter than most of the women he fooled around with, though he never seemed to realize that fact."

Groucho asked her, "You think these gonifs were pressuring him about something?"

"Probably," she answered, "but I have no idea what it was."

He said, "You've been working on script for *The Legend of King Arthur.*"

"Until Brian Montaine kicked off, yes. Now those halfwits at Paragon aren't sure what they're going to do." She started walking back toward her deck chair. "My specialty for years has been coming in after several no talent hacks have screwed up a screenplay and fixing the damn thing. I'm a hell of a good script doctor."

"Interesting that Brian Montaine and Dr. Benninger both shuffled off in the same week." He followed her around the pool. "And you knew them both."

"What are you suggesting—that I committed a double murder?" She laughed again and sat down.

He stopped a few feet from her, locked his hands behind his back. "You're not attending Montaine's burial festivities?"

She scowled. "Funerals are a stupid ritual and I wouldn't be caught dead at one." She paused, then made a chuckling noise. "There's a witty remark you might want to use."

"I already have," he assured her.

Twelve

I stepped out of the rainy morning into the Seaside Café.

Behind the counter Enery was serving a plate of waffles and pork sausage to a cowboy bit player, in costume, who was hunched on a stool.

In one of the booths a midget couple were arguing in whispers, glowering at each other and ignoring their breakfasts.

"You better not try to upstage me again, schmuck," the little blonde warned.

Enery nodded in the direction of the sixth, and most distant, booth. He lifted his left shoulder slightly, looking concerned. "Want anything, Frank?"

"Just coffee." I stopped, leaned an elbow on the counter. "I'll get a cup here and carry it back with—"

"I'll bring it."

I grinned. "I probably won't need protection, but okay, thanks."

The police detective, from the look of him sitting down far back in the booth, just made the height requirements for the Bayside force. He was thickset and dark.

"I'm Frank Denby." I slid in opposite him.

"Leo Conway," he said, voice low. "I've only got a few minutes."

"Okay, fine." I clasped my hands together and rested them on the tabletop.

Detective Conway had a pack of Lucky Strikes resting on the table next to his rain-spotted hat. "You're looking into the Benninger killing," he said. "You and Groucho Marx."

"That's right. Do you have—"

"You've got to be damn careful."

"Is this a warning to lay off?"

"No, Denby, it's a warning about Branner. He knows—" He stopped talking when Enery delivered my cup of coffee.

"Everything going right, Frank?" asked the actor.

"Seems to be."

"I'll be right over there." He started walking away.

The midget couple was still arguing and Enery halted beside their booth.

"How about refills on the coffee, folks?"

"Scram," the man suggested.

I nodded at Conway. "What about Sergeant Branner?"

"The bastard knows you guys are nosing around and trying to get the London dame sprung."

"We're already aware of that."

"But you probably don't know why he's trying to scare you off." He rested his elbows atop the table, leaning forward.

"True," I agreed.

"Branner had some kind of deal going with the doctor."

"What sort?"

"Benninger was up to here in the dope racket."

"We've heard something about that. How did Branner tie in?"

"He was on the take, getting dough to see that nobody bothered the doctor."

"Benninger's practice was in Beverly Hills, he only lived in Bayside," I pointed out. "Did the sergeant see that he wasn't bothered at his office either?"

Conway nodded. "Yeah, Branner is damn good at arranging stuff like that, Denby."

"Who were the Beverly Hills cops in on the deal?"

"That I don't know."

I asked, "What about Tartaglia? Does he figure in this?"

The detective answered, "Sure, but Jack Cortez was the guy who dealt with the doctor."

"And did Cortez have something to do with his murder?"

Conway shook a cigarette out of the pack, rolled it around between his thumb and forefinger. "I don't know about that, but Cortez was the one who was supplying Benninger with dope to sell to his high-class customers," he said. "And Branner, that son of a bitch, was looking out for them."

I tapped the side of my coffee cup. "But you don't intend to mention this to anybody official."

"You're damned right I don't." He lit his cigarette. "But when Lefcowtiz—he's a pal of mine—mentioned what you were trying to do, I figured I'd better talk with you."

"What do you want out of this?"

"I'd like to see Branner get cut off at the knees," the detective replied. "And I wanted to let you know that he was gunning for you two guys."

"Can I contact you again if—"

"Hell no," he said. "You don't even know me, Denby, you've never met me." Gathering up his cigarette pack and his damp hat, he left the booth. "See you."

After Detective Conway had gone, Enery came back. "You all right?"

"All right, yeah, but watchful."

"The cop threaten you?"

"Nope, just passed on some helpful advice."

"Are you and Groucho messed up in something dangerous again?"

"It certainly seems like we are," I admitted.

After descending from his Beverly Hills interlude with Maddy Dubay, Groucho later told me, he drove down and parked his Cadillac on Doheny. He headed on foot for a favorite smoke shop of his. The rain was coming down in a misty drizzle.

He went loping along, hands in his trouser pockets and shoulders slightly hunched. When he pulled open the glass-paneled door of VANGELDER, TOBACCONIST, a small bell tinkled at the far end of the narrow shop.

The scents of cigars, pipe tobacco, and old smoke were thick in the air. VanGelder, a middle-aged man with a stubble of beard, was behind the counter.

"That's the worst case of five o'clock shadow we've had in these parts in years," observed Groucho.

The proprietor smiled. "Groucho, what a coincidence," he said. "Your brother was in here not a half hour ago."

"You'll have to be more specific," suggested Groucho. "At the time of the last census it was determined that I was in possession of four siblings. Technically that's known as a gaggle. And I'm sure that if you gaggle twice a day with warm water and salt, why, you'll be up and around in no time."

"It was the funny Marx Brother who was just here."

"I, sir, am the funny Marx Brother." He rose up briefly on his toes. "And I assure you I haven't set foot in this shabby firetrap in a week."

"No, I mean the Italian one. Chico. That's who it was. He—"

"Whatever you do, don't loan that man any money," warned Groucho, reaching across the counter and around the displays of pipes and lighters to clutch the owner's arm. "Oh, I know too well that, because of his glib banter and his sparkling Romanesque person, people often mistake him for Mussolini. Unlike that renowned dictator, however, Chico has never managed to get a single railroad to run on time and he has never paid back a loan. Unless he owed the money to some goniff who was in a position to attack his knees with a baseball bat."

The proprietor freed himself from Groucho's grip. "Chico bought a box of Dunhill Four-tens."

"My favorite smoke."

"He told me he was buying them as a present for you, Groucho."

He shook his head. "That wasn't Chico," Groucho assured him. "Chico hasn't bought a present for me since I was in swaddling clothes. And that's got to be, oh, at least eight or nine years ago."

VanGelder produced a box of Groucho's favorites and set it atop the glass counter. "Chico informs me that you're going to be making a new movie."

"Actually it will be a series of lantern slides entitled *Ten Nights in a Bar Room and Two Weeks in Traction.* I portray Little Egypt and perform the Dance of the Six Veils. Initially it was intended to be the Dance of the Seven Veils but our director, noneother than D. W. Griffith, saw me in the all together and suggested that I keep at least one veil—preferably of a strongly opaque nature—on during the entire proceedings."

"Your brother said the movie is going to be called *Room Service*." VanGelder wrapped the box of cigars in dark green paper. "What's it about?"

"About a hooker who makes house calls," explained Groucho. "I was going to star as her pimp, but then the International Brotherhood of Pimps, Panderers, and Procurers lodged a formal complaint. They claimed I'd dishonor their profession."

"I'm sure it'll be funny." He handed Groucho the package.

"Faith is a marvelous thing." Groucho rolled his eyes heavenward, paid for his purchase, and left the shop.

He was planning to stroll over to Chasen's restaurant on nearby Beverly Boulevard for an early lunch. After Groucho had covered less than a block, a very attractive blonde stepped out of the recessed doorway of an antique shop.

"Would you be Groucho Marx?"

"Not if I had any choice," he answered, stopping. "But by now the name is on all the towels and silverware and it's just too much trouble to change it." His eyes narrowed and he scrutinized the approaching young woman. "You look moderately familiar, my dear. Did I make some sort of lewd advance toward you on a prior—"

"Oh, nothing like that, Mr. Marx. I'm simply a great fan of yours." From her large black shoulder bag she withdrew a nine-by-twelve-inch manila envelope. "Would you do me a really big favor and autograph this photo for me?"

"Of course, my pet." He gave her one of his moderately leering smiles. "Let me step over under the protection of yon awning so the ink won't run." He trotted over to the doorway and under the shelter of the candy-striped antique shop awning.

90

He slid the photo free and turned it over. "Oy, not a very flattering shot."

The glossy photograph showed a corpse lying on a slab. Someone had scrawled a crude moustache on the dead man's face. Printed across the lower half of the picture were the words— THIS IS YOU IF YOU DON'T FORGET ABOUT FRANCES LONDON!

"A very poignant invitation to develop amnesia, but I'm afraid I'm not going to quit." He looked up and realized that the blonde had long since departed.

"Darn, every time I meet a really nice-looking girl, she turns out to have some flaw or other." Shaking his head, he very carefully returned the threatening picture to its envelope and folded both away inside his coat.

He decided to cancel his lunch plans.

Thirteen

The Hollywood Memorial Park cemetery is on Santa Monica Boulevard, just about on top of the Paramount studios. In addition to Valentino, quite a few other silent movie stars are interred there, including Barbara LaMarr, Renee Adoree, and Theodore Roberts. There are a lot of impressive tombstones, vaults, mausoleums, and, this being Hollywood, palm trees.

The afternoon of Brian Montaine's funeral service there were also several hundred fans, tourists, and onlookers crowding the acre of lawn that fronted the Chapel of the Pines. Cops were dotting the gray, rainy cemetery grounds and keeping the crowd at a distance. Black umbrellas rose up all around.

Jane made her way up the gravel pathway toward the chapel. It was a long, low stucco building with slanting red tile roofs. There were several large palm trees in front of it and a stand of pines behind.

A pair of uniformed policemen framed the entryway and just behind them loomed a large fat man in tailcoat and striped trousers. He scanned Jane, obviously unable to recognize her as anyone.

She took out the invitation her friend, Dianne Sayler, had

sent her and handed it to him.

He read it, smiled a minimal smile, and said, "Go on in, miss."

Nearly all the pews were already occupied. The gray day gave an odd glow to the stained glass windows.

As Jane hesitated on the threshold, Conrad Nagel spotted her and got up from his seat to hurry over to her.

"Miss Danner, isn't it?" the dapper blond actor asked.

"Yes, but I'm afraid I don't recognize—"

"Conrad Nagel. I was the master of ceremonies at the premiere of *The Pirate Prince* at Klein's Babylonian a few months ago," he explained quietly.

"Oh, yes, that's right. I remember you now, Mr. Nagel."

"Your friend, Groucho Marx, disrupted the whole evening," he whispered, obviously still unhappy about it.

"Yes, but to catch a killer," she reminded him.

Nagel adjusted the carnation he was wearing in his lapel, then glanced around the crowded chapel and at the open doorway. "You're not planning to do anything like that here today, are you?"

"Not that I know of," she told the uneasy actor. "Of course, Groucho can be extremely unpredictable and so you can never—"

"I have the honor of having been invited to deliver the major eulogy for my dear friend, Brian Montaine." Nagel looked around again. "I would hate to think that Groucho Marx was intending to disrupt my—"

"Don't worry, Mr. Nagel," Jane advised him. "Even if Groucho does burst in—I'm almost certain he'll wait until you've spoken your piece." She smiled, eased around him, and seated herself at one of the few remaining vacant spots.

Outside the crowd murmured loudly and a few people shouted.

A moment later Errol Flynn, with a very young blond girl on his arm, entered the chapel and started down the aisle toward the seats that were being held for him. He paused on his way to shake hands with David Niven and Cesar Romero and then to kiss Dolores Del Rio on the cheek.

Jane found herself next to a middle-size, heavyset man.

"Don't let Nagel intimidate you," he told her.

"He'd have to be about six inches taller and about fifty percent a better actor before he'd have much chance of doing that."

"I'm Edward Arnold," he said. "I have a hunch you didn't recognize me."

"I don't go to the movies very often."

Someone tapped her on the shoulder.

Dianne, all in black, was standing in the aisle and leaning close to her. "I'm awfully glad you showed up, Jane," she whispered. "I can't talk to you now, but can you meet me afterward?"

"Sure, of course. Tell me where, Dianne."

"About a block from here, a dismal little dump called the Scenario Bar and Grill."

"I know where it is, yes."

Very close to Jane's ear, the widow said, "I'll tell you what really killed Brian." She touched her shoulder and returned to the front of the chapel.

The Elm Hotel was in downtown Los Angeles, a couple of run-down blocks from Pershing Square. While Groucho was skipping lunch and Jane was attending the funeral, I was checking with an old informant from my *LA Times* days.

The small lobby of the five-story Elm had green linoleum on the floor. There was a very old sofa, three chunky armchairs, two sand ashtrays, and three floor lamps with sailboats in the sunset shades. I had two similar lamps in my furnished cottage and when I saw these, I had a brief vision of a vast factory somewhere with sailboats in the sunset shades rolling along on huge conveyor belts.

The lobby had recently been sprayed for bugs and that smell partially masked the older odors of stale food, dead cigarettes, and bad plumbing.

A fat man wearing ragged tweed slacks and a faded USC sweatshirt was dozing in one of the chairs. A copy of *The Saturday Review of Literature* lay steepled on the linoleum just below his dangling left hand.

A plump orange cat was sprawled on the arm of the sofa and he growled at me and swatted at the air as I headed by him toward the desk.

No clerk was on duty. On the countertop a long line of ants was marching toward an abandoned coffee cup.

The single elevator didn't inspire confidence, so I decided to climb the two floors to Tim O'Hearn's room.

The stairways weren't carpeted either, but they also lacked linoleum. The odors were about the same as down in the lobby except there wasn't any bug spray to hide them.

Somebody had been sick about five feet short of my informant's door. I skirted that, continued on, and then stopped and knocked on 213.

From inside the room organ music welled up and Harry Whitechurch's voice, more somber than it was on our radio show, said, "And now it's time for *The Search for Love*, the true-life story of a young widow's courageous quest for happiness. Brought to you today and every day by Bascom's One-Hundred-Percent Soap. If you want pure soap, then—" The radio suddenly died.

"Yeah?" inquired O'Hearn on the other side of the room's thin door.

"It's Frank."

The door opened a few inches and a thin, faded man of about fifty squinted out at me. "Oh, yeah, hi, Frank." O'Hearn had a brown bottle of Lucky Lager Beer in his hand. "Come on in, but excuse the looks of the place. I split up with Agnes, you know, and this new dump lacks a woman's touch."

All the shades were down and a small electric heater glowed in front of the wide door that hid the wall bed. There was one armchair and it was piled high with movie trade journals, racing forms, and tip sheets. About a half dozen paper plates were scattered around, sitting on the linoleum, resting on the bureau, shoved behind the chair. The plates held the remnants of cheese sandwiches that were splotched with mold of varying hues.

"My temperature is all screwed up." O'Hearn seated himself in one of the two metal folding chairs his room possessed. "That's why I got the damn heater going full blast. I'm going to have to talk to a doctor, find out how low your temperature can drop before you're just simply dead and done for."

"What's your temperature now?"

"I can't exactly tell because I broke my thermometer about three weeks ago." He nodded at the other folding chair.

I sat, facing him. "What have you found out, Tim?"

"Fifteen bucks worth."

"Too much," I told him, noticing that there was another decaying cheese sandwich beneath my chair.

97

"There's this recession going on." He paused to drink from the beer bottle. "Besides, Frank, gathering the kind of info you want is extremely risky."

"Ten bucks."

"Twelve."

"Nope, ten or I go drop in on Terry Wollter."

"That stumblebum? He doesn't even know which end to put his hat on." O'Hearn sampled the Lucky Lager once more. "All right, since we're old pals. Make it ten bucks."

I nodded. "Okay, fine. Now what about—"

"I need the ten up front, Frank."

I took a five-dollar bill out of my wallet, handed it to him. "*Five* in front."

Muttering, he leaned and snatched the money. "First, I'll give you some advice for free," he said, crumpling the bill and stuffing it in the pocket of his coat sweater. "Even other guys in the Combination are leery of Tartaglia. He's, you know, like Bugsy Siegel. Crazy and mean."

"What about Jack Cortez?"

O'Hearn tilted his head to the left and twisted his lips. "Not as nutty as Tartaglia, but a nasty son of a bitch. He isn't somebody you want to annoy, Frank."

"Be that as it may, what have you found out?"

O'Hearn finished the beer and set the empty bottle on the floor near a lineup of other empty bottles. "Dr. Benninger was doing business with Tartaglia," he said. "Jack Cortez was the guy he actually dealt with directly, the one who supplied him with what he needed and the one he paid off to."

"Did they have anything to do with Benninger's getting killed?"

"I'm working up to that angle," my informant answered.

98

"What I'm hearing—and keep in mind I have to be damn careful how I nose around on this, Frank—the word I'm getting is that the doctor was pretty upset about something maybe three four days before he got bumped off."

"About what?"

O'Hearn frowned. "I think Jack Cortez was pressuring him to do them some kind of favor."

"Such as?"

"I'm trying to find out."

"Suppose he refused to do what they wanted—would they kill him over that?"

"Hell, Tartaglia would have you killed if you sang 'The Star Spangled Banner' off-key," answered O'Hearn. "Lots of times he'd kill you for no reason at all. I told you, the guy's nuts."

I inched my chair closer to his. "How about Frances London? Who set her up?"

"The consensus is she didn't have anything to do with killing Benninger."

"That's our opinion, too, Tim," I reminded him. "What I'm paying you for is some details we can use to help her."

"Not much yet on that," he said, shaking his head.

"Are Tartaglia and Jack Cortez tied in with framing her?"

Getting up, O'Hearn scanned his room. "I had another bottle of beer someplace," he said, starting to search.

"Who framed her?" I asked him.

"Well, I did hear one thing, but I'm not sure if you can put much faith in it, Frank." Down on his knees, he was sweeping a hand along under the bureau. "She's got an agent, doesn't she?"

"Yeah, it's a guy named Nate Winston."

"You should maybe talk to him." He made a chuckling noise

and stood up clutching a bottle of warm beer. "Now we have to find the church key."

I left my chair. "What about Winston?"

"Her agent?" He shrugged. "There's a possibility he's not exactly kosher." He spotted a bottle opener atop the bureau next to a battered Betty Boop doll. "That's all I heard about him."

I gave him another five-dollar bill. "I'll talk to you again tomorrow, Tim."

He nodded as he pried the bottle cap off. "Okay, but let's all be circumspect about this, huh? I really don't want to annoy Tartaglia or anybody who works for him."

"We share that goal," I assured him and left his room.

A block and a half from the hotel, I found a telephone booth that somebody hadn't been sick in. Stepping in, I dropped my nickel and called the office of Frances London's agent.

"Hollywoodland Answering Services," answered a young woman after the second ring.

"I want to get in touch with Nate Winston."

"You and a heck of a lot of other people, including three bill collectors and a couple ex-wives."

"I'm with MGM," I lied, "and we're very interested in one of his clients."

"Boy, there's something you don't hear often. MGM interested in anybody that bum represents," she said. "Well, you're out of luck."

"And why is that?"

"He seems to have skipped town," said the answering service operator. "Nobody around here knows where the heck the guy is and he sure didn't tell us. Some people think he's maybe in

Mexico, others favor Canada. Me, I have no opinion."

"Well, if he does contact you, tell him to get in touch with Louis B. Mayer."

"Sure thing," she said, laughing and breaking the connection.

Fourteen

The only other patron in the shadowy, early afternoon Scenario Bar & Grill was a sad, pale man who might've been F. Scott Fitzgerald.

He looked up briefly from his drink when Jane and Dianne Sayler came in, then returned his attention to the envelope he'd been scribbling on with a fat black fountain pen.

Jane said to her friend, "We've got some privacy now. Explain what you meant about how Brian really died."

"I have to lead up to that. Let's sit down and get a drink first." Dianne led her over to a booth. "The Scenario is basically a dump," she said, sitting. "And they keep it so air-conditioned that icicles tend to form on your butt, but it's close to the cemetery."

"I suppose they cater to the after-funeral crowd."

Her friend asked, "What'll you have?"

"Just a glass of seltzer."

The artist waved in the direction of the husky redheaded bartender. "Rudy," she called, "the usual and a plain soda."

The big freckled man waved back, nodding. "Long time no see, kid," he said. "On the wagon were you?"

"No, simply hitting a better class of saloon." She leaned back against the dark-paneled wall of their booth.

"That's what I like about this town," observed Rudy. "Everybody is a wiseass, if you'll pardon my French."

Jane unfastened her hat. "I hate these things," she said, taking it off and setting it on the table.

"I'm glad you showed up for the funeral, Janey."

"You're the only one who calls me that anymore."

"I won't if you'd prefer Jane."

"No, it's fine. Reminds me of my innocent school girl days."

"I'd have to go back even further than that to dredge up any memories of my innocent days." She frowned at the bartender as he delivered their drinks. "Still the slowest service in Hollywood, I notice."

Rudy chuckled. "How come I never see your pictures in the *Saturday Evening Post*?"

"Because I work for *Collier's* and the *Post* won't use anyone who works for them."

"So that's why I never spot any of Norman Rockwell's stuff in *Collier's*."

"Right, exactly, it's a conspiracy and I'm thinking about staging a sit-down strike."

"Naw, you don't want to go all the way back to Philly just to sit down. It's a dull town. Way I see it, you—"

"Rudy, you can go away now," suggested Dianne.

"Okay, I don't want to outwear my welcome." He headed back for the bar.

"He really babbles a lot." Dianne picked up her Tom Collins. Jane said, "You ready to talk now?"

After glancing over at Rudy and then the pale man who was probably F. Scott Fitzgerald, her friend said, "Your boyfriend—

Fred Denby, isn't it?"

"Frank Denby."

"I heard he was some kind of detective—Oh, by the way, what's the guy look like? Tall and handsome?"

"Middle-size and passable, but I love him," answered Jane. "He's actually a radio writer, Dianne, but he does some amateur detective work now and then. He and—"

"He and Groucho Marx. Yes, that was in all the papers last fall."

"Right now they're looking into the murder of that plastic surgeon, Dr. Benninger who—"

"That's funny." The artist had been reaching for her drink, but she stopped, frowning.

"In what way?"

Dianne answered, "I'll get to that, Janey, but let me backtrack a little first." She drank about half her drink. "I never talked much about my reasons for splitting with Brian. It isn't the sort of thing I wanted to see in columns. He was—and it had been going on for at least a year before I decided that I couldn't help him and he wasn't going to help himself—Anyway, Brian was pretty seriously involved with heroin."

"Is that where Dr. Benninger fits in?"

Dianne blinked. "How'd you know that?"

"Something Frank found out. The doctor was supplying drugs to some of his patients."

"Yes, Brian was one of them," she said. "It fouled up our marriage but, so far it hadn't much screwed up his career."

"Did anyone at Paragon know about his problem?"

"Sure, the Zansky Brothers and their chief troubleshooter, a guy named Tad Ballard," answered Dianne. "Probably a few others. Every damn one of those costume epics Brian starred in made money for Paragon, so they put up with his habit and covered for him." She finished her Tom Collins. "Keep in mind, Janey, that none of them tried to get him off heroin. They just made damn sure he stayed in good enough shape to get in front of the cameras." She waved again at the bartender. "You may not keep up with crap like this, but Brian's been on the list of the top ten box-office draws for the past three years—ever since he made *The Sword of Charlemagne*. An actor with that much pull, you treat very well and you overlook his weaknesses."

Rudy brought over a fresh Tom Collins. "I just realized why you're wearing black," he said to Dianne. "Your husband died and today was his funeral. Sorry I didn't think of that earlier. This one's on the house, kid."

"Thanks," she said. "But he was on his way to being my *former* husband."

"Sorry anyway." He went away.

Jane poked at an ice cube that was floating at the top of her glass of seltzer. It went sinking to the bottom and then bobbed up again. "Brian didn't actually die of a heart attack, did he?"

"No, he didn't." She seemed to be having a little trouble breathing. After grabbing hold of the edge of the table with both hands, she took a slow deep breath in and out. "Brian's valet found him sprawled on the floor in his den when he came home after his night off. That's Edwin, a very savvy Hollywood servant. He realized that Brian had died from a heroin overdose—hell, the needle was still sticking in his backside. Anyway, Edwin didn't call Brian's doctor or the police."

"He telephoned this Tad Ballard, the Paragon trouble-shooter?"

"That's right, Janey, yes. Ballard's by way of being a sort of garbage man, an expert at cleaning up messes," Dianne said after starting on her second drink. "He went over Brian's mansion, got rid of all the drug paraphernalia. Then he called in a physician who's on their payroll, a guy who helps them cover up the occasional suicide, drug accident, or bad case of wife beating." She leaned back again. "And that's how Brian came to die of a heart attack."

"How'd you find out what really went on?"

"Edwin dropped by early the next day," she replied. "He knew I probably wouldn't tell anyone or make a fuss. 'I simply thought, mum, that you'd like to know. Seeing as how you were once close to him.' "

Jane asked, "Do you want me to suggest to Frank that he look into this?"

"I haven't yet come to the part I've been really brooding about," Dianne said. "About two weeks ago Brian telephoned me—for the first time in months. He didn't sound all that well and he told me he'd decided, as soon as the shooting on *The Legend of King Arthur* was over, to check himself into a sanitarium and take a cure."

"He'd tried that before, hadn't he?"

The artist held up two fingers. "Twice, but the cures didn't take and he went back on the stuff," she said. "This time, though, he swore he was going to make it."

"If you came back and stuck with him through the ordeal?"

She nodded. "That was it, but I'd been through all that crap before and I told Brian so," Dianne said. "But then last week he called me again. He said he'd figured out a way to guarantee he'd stay off drugs. What he intended to do was go to the newspapers and publicly admit his habit. He was also planning to accuse Benninger and that bastard, Jack Cortez, of running a dope business that catered to show people."

"That wasn't smart."

"It wasn't, no, and I told him that." She tried her drink again. "Brian was a very frugal man and he'd invested in real estate for years. He wasn't really worried if his career in movies was ruined by his public confession. And he had the notion that he could buy extra protection for himself and keep Cortez from hurting him."

"But maybe they found out about what Brian was intending to do," Jane suggested. "Do you think Cortez might have had something to do with his death?"

Dianne said quietly, "That's what I want you to talk to your boyfriend about."

Fifteen

By sundown the rain had turned to mist and the stretch of Hollywood we were driving through had a fuzzy gray look. The windshield wipers of my yellow Plymouth coupé were making that odd keening noise they sometimes made on foggy nights.

"Once we get settled into our new digs," I said to Jane, "I'm seriously going to consider buying a new car. Not a brand-new car, but one that's somewhat newer than this one."

She'd been turned in the passenger seat, eyes slightly narrowed, looking again out the back window. "Hum?" she said.

"Hey, nobody's following us."

Sighting, she faced forward. "We disagree," she said quietly. "But I know darned well a huge black Pontiac has been trailing us off and on from the time you picked me up at my place."

Nodding at the rearview mirror, I said, "I've been checking that ever since you first mentioned it. I haven't noticed a damn thing."

"That's because these guys are tricky, Frank. They don't stay behind us every single minute."

"I took another look, still didn't see a tail. You're sure, huh?"

"Pretty near." She folded her arms under her breasts.

"I didn't think I'd found out enough about anything to make me dangerous to anyone."

"From what I hear, this Tartaglia doesn't require much in the way of motivation."

On our left we passed a movie palace that was showing *Jezebel.* "Bette Davis strikes again," I observed.

"She's okay," said Jane. "It's George Brent I don't much care for. He's always just George Brent."

"No, sometimes he's George Brent clean-shaven and sometimes he's George Brent with a moustache."

"That's your idea of a wide dramatic range, huh?"

Up ahead loomed Moonbaum's, the delicatessen where we were going to meet Groucho. "Well, Brent's better than Henry Fonda."

"No, he isn't. Fonda's cute and boyish."

"The perennial ingenue."

"You don't like him because he's taller than you."

I spotted a parking space a quarter of a block down from the restaurant. "Parking in Hollywood is difficult work, miss," I explained, slowing. "No verbal attacks until we're safely in the space. Okay?" I took another look back, but saw no sign of the black car Jane'd seen.

"Telling the truth isn't technically a verbal attack."

"Nobody tells the truth in this part of California. Do you want to be a misfit?"

A silvery Rolls honked at me while I was maneuvering into the spot. Then a plump gray-haired lady in a rattletrap Ford gave me the finger as she went swerving around me.

"I'm going to quit arguing with you about your failings," promised Jane. "I realized that you're simply trying to distract me from the fact that we've got goons keeping an eye on us."

Snug in the space, I turned off the key and set the brake. "We've arrived." I stepped out of the car on the street side.

Before I could head for the sidewalk to open the door on Jane's side, a big black Pontiac came roaring out of the mist behind us.

I dived back toward my coupé.

The big car missed hitting me by about seven or eight inches, a foot at the most.

"Jesus." I found I was having trouble breathing and my heart seemed to be beating at several new spots.

"Frank, are you okay?" Jane came running around the car to me. She took hold of me, the way you do when you want to keep somebody from falling down.

I guess I looked like I was a good candidate for falling down.

"I'm fine, yeah." My voice had an animated cartoon quality to it.

She shook her head. "I don't think you are. People who are okay don't turn that deathly shade of white."

After concentrating on my breathing for nearly a minute, I admitted to her, "You were right about that damn car, Jane."

"I was. Did it touch you at all?"

"Nope, no. I dodged it."

"Maybe they intended to do that. Only wanted to scare you."

"They were terrifically successful."

From the sidewalk someone called, "Are you two romantic leads going to carry this public display of affection any further or can I continue on my way to the neighborhood peepshow? If there's going to be any more hugging and smooching, then I'll stick around until—"

"Quit being a schmuck, Groucho," Jane, angry, suggested. "Those bastards came close to running him down."

Groucho came trotting out to our side of the car. "I missed that part of it," he told us. "Are you injured, Rollo?"

"No, just unsettled."

He nodded. "Which bastards would this be, Jane?"

She frowned at him. "Somebody you two have annoyed with your Pinkerton act I imagine," she said. "They followed us from my place."

"No specific idea who they were, Frank?"

I pointed toward the safety of the sidewalk. "Let's get clear of the traffic," I suggested. "I'm still feeling like a target."

Thoughtfully, as he stepped up onto the sidewalk, Groucho said, "This makes for an interesting coincidence, children."

"What does?" I was feeling wobbly, but by holding on to Jane I got out of the street.

"I had the distinct impression, as I tooled down here from my palatial manse, that I was being followed, too," he explained. "Although nobody tried to turn me into paving material."

"You two are obviously antagonizing somebody," said Jane.

"I antagonize just about everyone." Groucho lead us toward the restaurant door. "But since Franklin here is the next best thing to a saint, these vehicular interludes must have something to do with the murder."

As we entered Moonbaum's, Jane said, "There may be two murders, Groucho."

He halted on the white tiles of the restaurant foyer and went up on his toes, eyebrows climbing. "What are you saying, my child?"

She patted my shoulder. "Frank will explain."

Sixteen

Handing out mimeographed menus, our gaunt waiter was saying, "You'd be perfect to star in my play, Groucho. It's a comedy set in a delicatessen and is entitled *The Rape of the Lox.*"

"Don't tell me, Ira," urged Groucho. "I bet you want me to play the part of a dashing, quick-witted waiter."

Ira Mellman snapped his fingers. "That's it exactly," he said. "But this is more than the usual low slapstick you and your brothers have gotten trapped into doing."

"It's also profound I'll wager."

Ira snapped his thin fingers again. "You see, Groucho, this waiter is not only a master of verbal wit, he also has a miraculous effect on all the people he comes in contact with. Changes their lives for the better."

"It's *The Passing of the Third Floor Back* with laughs."

"That's it, right." He leaned closer to our booth, lowering his voice. "We hint, subtly, that he might be some sort of supernatural being."

I inquired, "How much of this play have you got written?"

He held up a single finger. "So far the first act," he answered. "But it's socko, Frank."

"How's the pastrami tonight?" asked Groucho.

"Same as always. Mediocre."

"I'll have the brisket."

"Wise choice. And you, miss?"

"Just coffee."

He gave Jane a disappointed look, but wrote her order on his pad. "Frank?"

"I hate to bring up the topic again. But lox. With cream cheese on rye."

"I'm not showing my play to anyone until it's finished. So you can relax until then." Bowing in Jane's direction, he headed for the kitchen.

Only about half the pale green booths were occupied so far. Directly across the restaurant from us a pair of blond identical twins were having blintzes.

Groucho rested his unlit cigar on the heavy glass ashtray. "Before we get to this other murder, Rollo," he said, "I must pass on a message from our gifted director, Annie Nicola. She telephoned me about an hour ago."

"Colonel Mullens's birthday party?" I asked. "I thought we didn't have to attend unless we—"

"Heavenly days, you're positively psychic, young feller."

"You always get that particular pained expression on your face when you're about to talk about the Colonel,"

His nod of agreement was forlorn. "According to Annie, who got it from the top executives at the pudding plantation, we absolutely have to attend this shindig tomorrow night, Frank."

"Why exactly?"

"The entire pudding team from Batten, Barton, Blinken and Nod—or whatever those advertising scoundrels from the East call themselves—will be arriving here in the Sunshine State tomorrow morning. Colonel Mullens thinks it would be just delightful if I were to perform a few ditties for the assembled multitudes at his shivaree."

"What's bad about that?" asked Jane. "You love to inflict your singing on people."

"I prefer to use my God-given voice, Little Nell, only to entertain those I consider deserving of such a treat," he countered. "And not to waste it on pudding mavens,"

I asked, "But you're going?"

"Annie mentioned that she's heard a rumor—and I hesitate to worry you babes in the wood with this news—that our Hooper ratings have been slipping the past few weeks."

"How bad is it?"

"If this were a horse race, Rollo, Jack Benny and Edgar Bergen would be a considerable way up the track from us."

Jane rested her elbow on the tabletop. "So you fellows are expected to butter up the Colonel and the visiting ad men?"

"That's a polite way of describing our shame, my dear," he acknowledged. "Oh, and dear little Polly is going to be in attendance, too, and it has been suggested that we perform a duet."

Jane grinned. "That news must've scared the heck out of Nelson Eddy and Jeanette MacDonald."

"Eddy's already gone into hiding and will only come out to answer requests to sing 'Short'nin' Bread,' " said Groucho. "As you may recall, Franklin, the Colonel is taking over the entire King Neptune Playland at the beach in your beloved Bayside for tomorrow night's funfest. He's invited three hundred of Hollywood's finest—Well, actually he could only find twenty-six who qualified as finest. The rest are the usual movie industry lowlifes. We are expected to be there no later than seven.

I glanced at Jane. "Want to come along? It looks like I'm

really going to have to attend this thing."

"Would you mind I don't?" she asked. "I want to work on getting another week of my strip done."

"Sure, that's okay."

"I'll arrange for you to meet one of the ladies from the Hula Hula Pavilion, Rollo, should you require female companionship," promised Groucho. "And now let's turn to a lighter topic. What second murder?"

"Jane went to Brian Montaine's funeral this afternoon."

He nodded at her. "Frank told me you're an old school chum of Dianne Sayler, the grieving widow."

Jane said, "I knew Dianne in art school and I've seen her occasionally since. We're not close, but she wanted to talk to me about Brian's death. And we did that after the services."

Groucho leaned forward, frowning. "Does she suspect her husband was murdered, too?"

"She doesn't," I put in. "But we think it's a strong possibility."

"How so?"

"Apparently Brian Montaine had a serious longtime heroin problem," she answered. "He was getting his drugs from—"

"None other than the respected Dr. Benninger." Groucho extracted his notebook from out of a side pocket of his checkered sport coat.

"You knew that already?" I asked.

"Picked it up from chatting poolside with the personable Maddy Dubay." He opened the notebook. "A very distracting name, I might add. I keep thinking it ought to mean something in Pig Latin."

"Do you also know," Jane asked him, "that Brian had resolved to quit using the stuff?"

"Nope, that news item Dracula's Daughter didn't impart to me while passing out the hemlock highballs."

"He was planning to make his addiction problem public, tell everybody what he'd been doing and where he got the stuff," continued Jane. "But before he could do that, he died instead."

"Not from a heart attack?" asked Groucho.

"Dianne didn't say anything about its being murder. She figures it was an overdose or a fatal reaction to the drug."

"Where'd she get that quaint notion?"

Jane filled him in about the actor's being found dead by his valet, about the subsequent cover up by the Paragon studio people. "Frank and I talked this over, Groucho, and we're wondering if somebody didn't arrange that overdose."

I said, "Murdering the guy and making it look like he'd killed himself accidentally—that would sure as hell keep him from talking."

Groucho leaned back, eyeing the plaster ceiling of the restaurant. "Benninger was very agitated and nervous during his last days on earth," he said slowly. "Could it be he knew about the plans to have Brian Montaine do a shuffle off? Could it even be that his pals in the drug trade had requested him to see to the chore of dispatching the actor?"

Jane sat up. "You think Dr. Benninger may've been involved in Brian's death?"

"It's an interesting possibility, my dear."

"Then who killed the doctor?"

"Possibly somebody from the firm of Tartaglia and Cortez," suggested Groucho. "Or maybe someone we don't even know about."

"Speaking of those unorthodox pharmacists," I put in. "I'm

betting they're the ones who put sinister black automobiles on our tails."

"Ah, that reminds me." Groucho extracted a folded sheet of paper from amidst the pages of his notebook and handed it across to me. "I'd advise you not to take a gander at this, Jane. It's a nasty billet-doux that was delivered to me whilst I was exiting my tobacconist's this afternoon."

"A threat?" I unfolded the sheet.

It was the morgue shot of the corpse with a Groucho moustache added.

He said, "Like all good advertisements, it's clear and to the point."

"Let me see." Jane took the picture from me. "Whoever did this sure isn't much of a letterer. Doesn't draw moustaches all that well either."

"To cause my grizzled locks to stand on end, my dear, you don't have to be a Daumier—or even a Rube Goldberg."

"How'd they," I inquired, "get this thing to you, Groucho?"

"A very comely blond lass hand-delivered it and then vanished like a . . ." He stopped talking, tilting his head back. "What was it Edison cried out when he discovered the lightbulb?"

"Now I've got something to put in all those empty sockets?" I suggested.

"Eureka?" said Jane.

"That's it," said Groucho. "I knew it was the name of some little California town. Eureka, then. My aging old brain has just now remembered where I saw that lass before."

"You recognized the girl who gave you this thing?"

Ira had arrived with our coffee. "I just now thought up a great opening scene for my second act," he told Groucho.

"You might want to consider making your opus a one-act

118

extravaganza, my boy." He pulled his cup of coffee closer to him, making a shooing motion with his other hand. After the waiter had bowed at Jane and gone shuffling off, Groucho continued. "This winsome blonde had apparently been tracking me though the byways of Beverly Hills. She lurked in an antique shop doorway and thrust this crude missive upon me. I had the impression at the time that I'd seen her before, but couldn't place her."

"But now you can?" Jane asked.

"I had a feeling she reminded me of someone," he answered. "The resemblance isn't all that strong, but it's there. She looks somewhat like Frances London—or like Frances did in her heyday."

"Know her name?"

He shook his head. "She's a would-be actress—and only her vague resemblance to Frances, coupled with a chronic lack of talent, has hobbled her career on the silver screen," he said, absently stirring three spoonfuls of sugar into his coffee. "About a year ago she wangled an interview with my brother Zeppo—also known as the Solvent Rover Boy—at his talent agency. She was coming out of his office as I was going in and I remember commenting on her charming demeanor to Zeppo. Well, actually her charming bosom. If she hadn't been somewhat bundled up this afternoon, I'd had recalled her sooner."

"Would your brother remember her name after all this time?" I asked.

"I doubt he'll even remember who I am, but he can, hopefully, put me on the wench's tail. Which isn't a bad place to camp for the night." He took a sip of his coffee, winced.

Jane said, "If she looks something like Frances London and she's involved in this mess—could she also be the lady those witnesses thought was Frances banging on Dr. Benninger's door?"

"Aha! Or make that—Eureka!" Groucho straightened up out of his slouch. "You may just have had a brainstorm there, Nurse Jane." He frisked himself until he found his fountain pen and then scribbled a note on a blank page of his book. "One more thing to chat with the lady anent."

I mentioned, "She's probably working for Tartaglia."

"I'll keep that in mind and approach her with caution."

"There are some other people we have to approach," I said. "What's the name of Montaine's valet, Jane?"

"I only know his front-end name. That's Edwin. I can find out the rest and if he's still at Montaine's mansion in Bel Air."

"Also be illuminating to talk to the troubleshooter from Paragon. Was it Tad Ballard who got Montaine's possible murder passed off as a heart attack?"

Jane nodded. "Him, yes."

"I'd like to nominate that actress whose face the good doctor botched up," added Groucho. "Elena Stanton. A long shot, yet she certainly seems to have a dandy motive for not being fond of Dr. Benninger."

"If Frances London gets out on bail tomorrow," said Jane, "you ought to talk with her again."

"Gracious me," said Groucho, "we're all going to be as busy as the little elves who paint the wild flowers such lovely colors. Although now that the elves have joined the union, they're certain to be making better money than we are." He tried his coffee again, then gave up on it. "I'll handle tracking down the blond messenger and Tad Ballard. Him I used to know back when he was writing tripe for *The Hollywood Reporter*. Can you cover the others, Frank? Then, if we have time before tomorrow night's debacle, we can pay Frances a visit together."

I nodded. "Are you going to need me to write you some material for your performance at the Colonel's doings?"

"No," Groucho assured me, "I intend to depend entirely on divine inspiration."

Seventeen

Wearing white tennis togs and looking, in his opinion, quite virile, Groucho went trotting into his den at a few minutes after ten the next morning. Tucking his racket up under his arm, he rested his backside on the edge of his desk and picked up the phone.

He gave the operator a number and a moment later was talking to his brother Zeppo. "I'd like, Herbert, some information about . . . What do you mean that wasn't a cordial brotherly greeting? . . . Well, perhaps I could've opened with something like 'Hail to thee, O beloved brother,' but . . . No, I don't address Harpo as palsy-walsy. Who told you that I . . . Listen, Zeppo, I have a tennis date with Chaplin, so my time is . . . Well, Charlie Chaplin . . . No, I don't know whatever happened to Syd Chaplin. He was certainly very fetching in *Charley's Aunt*, but since it's his brother I'm about to face on the courts, I . . . No, I'm not lording the fact that I'm off to play tennis with Charlie Chaplin over you. Nor am I bragging about it . . . Well, when one of the world's best-loved comedians wants to play tennis, naturally he wants to be evenly matched. Therefore, he picked another beloved comic for an opponent and . . . I'm not implying that nobody loves you, Zeppo. Listen now. Do you remember that blond girl who looks like Frances London and has a singular pair of tsitskes? She was eager to have you represent her, this was about a year back and . . . Ah, right. That's her. Maggie Barnes. Do you know where I can find her and . . . No, I'm not contemplating adultery. Well, wait. I might be contemplating adultery—In fact, you could say that contemplating adultery has become one of my favorite hobbies of late and may even replace stamp collecting and making tie racks with my wood burning set as my favorite most pastime—but I am not contemplating adultery with Maggie Barnes. This has to do with a murder case I find myself working on. So if . . . How can I be getting senile at forty? . . . Okay, how can I be getting senile at forty-seven? Detecting is not a sign of mental decline. Being a crackerjack sleuth, I am obliged to solve a case now and then. It's my civic duty. So who represents Maggie Barnes? . . . Which goniff, Zeppo? . . . Rupe McClosky. I thought he only booked chimpanzees and trained fleas . . . Oh, he's trying to improve his image by adding bimbos like Maggie Barnes to his roster. Well, palsy-walsy, I appreciate your . . . No, I'm not being snide. I was simply expressing the bottled up feelings of fraternal devotion I have for you, my kid brother . . . Yes, I will say hello to Chaplin for you. Though I don't honestly believe he's looking for an agent. And now I must be going, Zep. Farewell."

He hung up, shifted his grip on his tennis racket, and went bounding out of the room.

Had he not tripped over a throw rug in the hall, it would've been a perfect exit.

The uniformed guard came out of the gatehouse that sat just to the right of the entrance to the private Malibu community I was visiting. He was large, wide, and tanned. "What's the name again?" He lifted his dark glasses to scan again the list of names on his clipboard.

"Frank Denby," I repeated, leaning my head out of the open window of my yellow coupé. "I have an appointment with Elena Stanton."

He moved a thick forefinger slowly along the list. "Could you be Fred Dimby?"

"What's it pay?"

He frowned at me briefly. "I mean, could that pinheaded swish who lives with her and off her have given me your name incorrectly? I've got a Fred Dimby down here to call on Miss Stanton at eleven o'clock."

"Yeah, that must be me."

"Your name's familiar." He made a check mark on the list, reached into the gatehouse, and tossed the clipboard onto his small desk.

"Which name?"

"Frank Denby. You connected with show business?"

"I write a radio show called *Groucho Marx, Private Eye.* Maybe you—"

"Can't stand the Marx Brothers." The guard gave a negative shake of his head. "I'll tell you who's funny, though. This guy Bob Hope. Have you seen *The Big Broadcast of 1938* yet?"

"Last week, sure. Hope is funny but not as funny as Groucho."

"He's funnier and he can sing."

"So can Groucho."

"Well, I never heard of your radio show, so I must know your name from someplace else." He thought for a moment. "*LA Times.* You wrote for them."

"Five years' worth."

"I read a lot of your stories." He stepped back into the gatehouse. "Hold on and I'll get the gate out of your way, Frank." He poked a button on a control panel.

The high wrought iron gates buzzed and rattled before slowly swinging inward.

"She lives in the big God-awful pink house on Lagunitas Way," he said.

I gave him a casual salute and drove on through the open gateway.

There were twenty-some homes scattered across the twenty-some acres inside the walls of this private community. Most of them were large and in Spanish or Moroccan style, with red tile roofs, cream-colored stucco exteriors, and quite a lot of black wrought iron trim. There were lots of palm trees, tropical plants and flowers, big stretches of bright green lawn. I thought I saw a peacock unfurling its tail amid the shrubbery, but I wasn't certain.

As I pulled into the drive of the former actress' sprawling pink house, a tall red-haired young woman, wearing a two-piece green swimsuit under a wide open white terry cloth robe, came striding across the splendid lawn of the mission-style house next door. She gave my car a brief glance that could best be described as disdainful, crossed the street, and started down the twisting wooden stairway that led to a wide stretch of private beach.

Today was sunny, though somewhat hazy, and a slightly fishy scent was drifting in from the Pacific Ocean on the warm late-morning wind.

"Are you Fred Dimby?" A very handsome man in white duck trousers and a crimson polo shirt had opened the wide redwood door of Elena Stanton's house while I was still several red tile steps from it.

"Frank Denby," I corrected, stopping just short of the fuzzy welcome mat.

"Close enough. C'mon in." He was tall, muscular in a life guard sort of way, and his shaggy hair was sun-bleached blond. "You recognize me, huh?"

"No." I stepped into the large hallway. The mosaic tile floor was turquoise, gold, and a sort of sandy red. "Actor?"

"Sure, I'm Gary LeMay."

"Not *the* Gary LeMay?"

"I'm not the kind of guy you maybe want to get too funny with, Denby," he advised. "Most recently I had a good part in *Ty-Gor's Hidden Treasure.*"

"Friend of mine was in that, too. Enery McBride."

"The colored boy," said the blond actor. "He's okay. Knows his place."

"Might I see Miss Stanton now?"

He leaned close to me. "She's had a very rough time," he told me. "Don't say anything to upset her, okay?"

"I'll sure try not to," I assured him. "But I do want to ask about Dr. Benninger, as I mentioned to her on the phone this morning."

"That son of a bitch," LeMay said. "You're not trying to find out who killed him, are you?"

"Nope, who didn't kill him."

"Then you must be trying to help Frances London."

"I am, along with Groucho Marx."

He said, "I worked on a quickie B movie with Frances once. *Frisco Female.* She's a very nice lady. You ever catch it?"

"Sure, Chester Morris was in that one."

"I played the gangster who gets tossed in the Bay in a bucket of cement."

"A memorable performance."

"I was pretty good in it," he said, starting away along the hall. "Let's go talk to Elena."

I felt as though I'd wandered into a chapter of a Republic Pictures serial, that I was imprisoned in the lair of some mysterious phantom. The living room had a shadowy underground feel to it. The full-length windows, all five of them were masked by thick, dark drapes and the only light came from the weak table lamp next to the deep armchair LeMay had escorted me to.

There were a lot of plants. Large wooden tubs held stunted palms, there were big coppery vases with overflowing ferns, spiky cactus and several things I couldn't identify but that looked like dwarf weeping willows. The room was chill and damp, smelling strongly of loamy earth.

Elena Stanton was in a high-backed white wicker chair. A thin woman, she sat very stiff and straight, wearing a long black dress. She also had a black scarf wound around so that it covered the lower half of her face. Her eyes were hidden by tinted glasses.

The blond actor was crouched on a gray hassock close by, holding her knobby right hand in both of his.

"I'm glad he's dead," she said in her pale, muffled voice. "I had nothing, however, to do with Benninger's death."

I leaned forward, thinking that it would help me hear her better. "Do you know any of his other patients? Anyone who ended up with a problem or a reason to hate the guy?"

The black scarf fluttered, very faintly, when she spoke. "He made several other mistakes besides mine. But I . . ." Her voice faded, the scarf grew still.

LeMay scowled at me. "She won't give you any of their names," he told me. "If any of that bastard's victims did kill him, she believes they were more than justified."

"You knew Frances London," I said to her. "Fact is, you made a picture together in 1933—*Midnight at the Castle.*"

"You remember seeing that?"

I admitted, "No, I never saw it. Just before coming over here I looked up your credits in a *Film Daily Year Book.*"

"It was a nice picture," she said.

"A big hit at the box office, too," added LeMay.

"The point I'm trying to make is that you knew Frances London and, hopefully, you liked her."

"I did, very much. Although I haven't seen her for years."

"She doesn't see many people anymore," put in the actor.

"We're trying to establish that she didn't have a damn thing to do with Dr. Benninger's death. To prove even a reasonable doubt, well, we need to have somebody else to suggest as the killer. We—that's Groucho Marx and I—don't want to frame anyone or cause them trouble, but if—"

"I can't help you with that," she told me. "But I invited you here because I do have something to tell you that may help poor Frances."

"Okay, fine." I leaned further forward.

"Benninger was more than just a plastic surgeon," she said. "He also supplied narcotics to quite a few Hollywood people."

I sat back. "We already knew that," I said. "Most of his stock was supplied by the outfit run by a guy named Tartaglia."

"And Jack Cortez," she added. "I met Cortez once when I was at a party with Benninger. A very attractive man, who hid his innate nastiness quite well."

"You don't need to tell him anything more." LeMay tightened his hold on her hand while giving me an unhappy scowl.

"It doesn't matter," she said. "Talking about that period

doesn't bother me, Gary." She paused, resting her head back against the high white wicker chair. "What Benninger did with some of the narcotics he handled—as he did in my case—what he did was provide painkillers to anyone who'd had an unfortunate accident while under his knife. After he ruined my face, there was considerable pain and, as you can imagine, much depression. He—"

"You should've sued the bastard," said LeMay, angry.

"I couldn't do that," she said quietly. "I was still a fairly successful actress then and I was hoping . . . Well, while Benninger was holding out hope that my face could be saved, he provided me with drugs to get me over the pain and the depression. Morphine, I found, works very well with pain and—"

"That's enough, Elena." Still holding her hand, LeMay stood up. "It hurts me when you talk about this stuff."

She got her hand away from him, patted his wrist gently. "It doesn't bother me," she assured him. To me she added, "It's my opinion, Mr. Denby, that Benninger's death had something to do with his involvement with people like Jack Cortez."

I rose. "Thanks for talking to me."

"I hope you get a chance sometime to see *Midnight at the Castle*," she said. "I was very pretty then."

"You were beautiful," said LeMay.

I left them there in the shadows.

Eighteen

The tourists, two of them, closed in on Groucho, as he later told me, a moment or so after he'd stepped out of his Cadillac onto the early afternoon sidewalk in the heart of Pasadena.

He was strolling along, unwrapping a fresh cigar, when the woman wobbled into his path. She was a large middle-aged lady in a print dress and she was carrying an autograph book. Her husband, a tall narrow man in a pale blue seersucker suit, lagged a few feet to the rear.

To avoid colliding with her, Groucho stopped dead, rose up on his toes, and took a hop backward. "Madam?"

"I think you're Groucho Marx," she explained, sounding nervous, "but my husband says you're somebody else."

He slipped the unwrapped cigar into the outer vest pocket of his jacket. "Actually, you're both right," he said, accepting the autograph album. "For many years I was Groucho Marx, but I eventually grew dreadfully tired of that. For over a month now I've been Tess of the d'Urbervilles. Truth to tell, madam, that's even less gratifying and I'm seriously considering becoming Tess of the Brown d'Urbervilles."

Perplexed, the woman watched him scribbling on a page of the fat book.

"And now I must continue on my appointed rounds." He returned the album, scooted around her, and moved off along the sidewalk.

After inspecting the inscription, she turned to him. "Merle, he went and signed it *Thomas Hardy.*"

"I told you it wasn't Groucho Marx."

Groucho walked to the middle of the block, slowed, then halted entirely. None of the buildings, neither the small shops nor the low office buildings, bore the address he was seeking. In the place where Maggie Barnes's agent ought to have his office, there was a narrow, rundown miniature golf course. The greens were overgrown and weedy, all the little windmills and arched bridges were faded and weather-beaten. The low picket fence that surrounded the Pee Wee Heaven Golf Park had numerous gaps and the swinging gate lay on its side at the edge of the gravel pathway. Two fat men, the only customers, were at the eleventh hole arguing.

There was a small gingerbread-covered cottage just inside the woebegone fence. "This must be the place where Hansel and Gretel moved after they retired," decided Groucho, entering the golf course and approaching the cottage.

When he knocked on the door, several more flakes of brittle yellow paint fell free and fluttered to the dry, balding doormat.

"Twenty-five cents," said the heavyset bald man who opened the door and handed a scorecard out to Groucho. "We're not too busy this afternoon and you can play right through, pal."

"It's tempting, since I do dearly love outdoor sports," said Groucho, taking out his cigar again. "But what I'm really seeking is Rupe McCloskey, the illustrious talent impresario. Can you direct me to his—"

"Hey, you're Groucho Marx." He snatched the scorecard back, tossed it away and shook Groucho's hand. "What sort of talent are you looking for, Groucho? I'll bet you need a leading lady for your next film. Come on in and we'll go through my book of star-caliber dames, I think I've got just the gal for *Room Service*."

"Alas, if only I'd known." Groucho slouched across the threshold. "As it is we're going to have to make do with Lucille Ball."

"An amateur, though her gams aren't bad. We can—watch your noggin, Groucho."

The ceiling was extremely low and Groucho had to duck down to avoid banging his head against one of the beams. "You run an intriguing business here, McCloskey," he told him. "It isn't every man who'd be shrewd enough to combine peewee golf with talent agenting."

"I'll be honest with you, Groucho." Hunched low, the agent walked over to his small desk and hunkered down behind it. "I got into miniature golf a bit late. Few years earlier a place like this would've done a land office business."

"Yes, that was about the same period when land offices were doing peewee golf business and pancakes were selling like hotcakes and all was right with the world except for a few isolated trouble spots in far-off Europe." He eyed the low ceiling and settled into a wooden chair that faced the agent's desk. "Didn't your offspring get mad when you borrowed their playhouse to use for your office."

"I'll be honest with you, pal," said McCloskey. "The people I bought this joint from were small."

133

Groucho lit his cigar, took a few puffs. "I'm looking for Maggie Barnes," he said, exhaling smoke.

"Maggie Barnes," said the agent. "Maggie Barnes. Nope, I can't place the name, Groucho."

"Sure you can, Rupe. You wouldn't want burly policemen with rubber hoses to have to come around asking you about her, would you?"

"What the hell's she done now?"

"How's extortion sound?"

"She tried to extort money from you?"

"No, but I would like to know how extortion sounds, McCloskey. I'm thinking of naming my new cat that." Groucho hunched, watching the agent's plump face. "I know that you do indeed represent the young lady. I also suspect that she's up to no good. On top of which, she might be able to supply me with some information."

McCloskey said, "I get it, Groucho. This is more of that amateur detective crap." He shook his head. "Let me tell you something, pal. You did okay on that Peg McMorrow mess, but you ought to rest on your laurels."

"I tried that, but it was very uncomfortable. Few people realize that laurels are extremely prickly," he said. "I'd like her address, Rupe."

"Maggie isn't acting anymore."

"On the contrary, I suspect she's played a couple of interesting roles very recently." He got up, moved to the desk and rested his left hand on it, palm down. "Where can I find her?"

"Take a look in the phone book, pal."

"I already did that, dear friend. She's not to be found in any of the directories for all of Greater Los Angeles."

"I'll be honest with you," the agent said. "I don't represent

Maggie any longer. We had a parting of the ways and—"

"Where is she?"

McCloskey swallowed once, glanced toward the tiny window on his right. "Not so loud, Groucho," he said, lowering his voice. "Suppose I gave you a tip on how to contract this broad? Would it be worth, say, fifty bucks?"

"Twenty-five."

"C'mon, I'm risking my neck here."

"How so?"

"She's tied in with a guy named Jack Cortez." His voice was even dimmer. "And Cortez works for—"

"That part I already know."

"I'm not going to put this in writing," said the agent, glancing again at the window. "I'll tell you the phone number and the address and *you* jot it down. Okay?"

Groucho drew out his notebook and then his fountain pen. "Dictate away, Rupe."

"What about the twenty-five clams?"

"After I have the information."

McCloskey made a surly noise, then said, "She lives in Santa Rita Beach. The address is three-oh-six Loma Vista Way, phone's Ocean fourteen-oh-five."

Groucho wrote that down, capped his pen, and shut the notebook. "If the lady isn't at home, Rupe, where else might I find her?"

The fat agent's sigh had a wheezy quality. "Don't tell anybody I told you this," he said. "Sometimes—things have been tough for Maggie lately, I hear—sometimes she works at a place in Bayside."

"A place frequented by lecherous sailors, wayward husbands, and callow college youths?"

"A whorehouse, yeah. This one's run by a lady calls herself Mrs. Ferguson."

"Who's bordello is it?"

"Word is it's one of Vince Salermo's," the agent answered. "But I hear Tartaglia may be a silent partner in this particular setup." Almost whispering, he gave Groucho the address.

"Is Maggie to be found there most nights?"

"Naw, she only works Fridays and Saturdays. So she'll be on duty tonight from about ten on."

Groucho put the notebook away and fetched out his wallet. "You've been a prince, Rupe." He gave him two tens and a five.

The agent snatched the bills, tucked then away in his pants pocket. "Could you get the hell out of here now, Groucho? I really don't want anybody to know you were talking to me."

"A lot of people seem to feel that way. Do you think I should start bathing in Rinso?"

The agent hurried over to the door and yanked it open. "Scram, please, huh?"

"I can take a hint." Groucho, after another puff on the cigar, crossed the small, low room. "You apparently want me to depart."

"But, hey," said McCloskey, "if you decide not to go with Lucille Ball, give me a jingle. I got just the dame for you."

Nineteen

No, it doesn't bother me," I said to Jane. "I've been doing this for months now, remember?"

"True, but since we're going to be moving into new quarters soon, I wanted to make sure."

I handed her another freshly washed soup bowl. "I haven't been helping with the household chores because I was trying to worm my way into your affections," I assured her as she dried the bowl with one of those embroidered dishtowels her aunt up in Fresno kept sending her.

"Some men, you know, resent housework, consider it beneath them."

"I don't know about them other fellers you've lived with, ma'am, but far as I'm concerned—and I can't speak for the other wranglers—I sure don't feel like no sissy 'cause I do these here dishes."

"There you go again, getting silly when I'm trying to be serious."

I passed her the saucepan I'd just scrubbed. "What you've got is opening night jitters," I suggested. "We've lived together peaceably since way last fall. Moving into a new and bigger house isn't going to affect how—"

"Up until now, though, you've had a separate house of your own and so have I," Jane persisted while drying the pan. "When we move next month, we'll be committed to *one* house. If you want to be by yourself for some reason, you won't have a spare place to go to. Neither will I."

I gestured in the direction of the Pacific Ocean with the hand that wasn't holding the sponge. "I can always sleep on the beach if we have a quarrel," I told her. "You aren't having second thoughts about this merger, are you?"

"No, but I want to make sure that you aren't."

Dropping the sponge in the sink, I wiped my hands on her dishtowel and then put them on her shoulders. I leaned and kissed her.

The phone in the living room commenced ringing.

We continued kissing for six more rings and then I moved back and away. "Better answer."

I picked it up on the ninth ring. "Okay," I said.

"Hello, Frank, how are you?"

"I'm okay, Polly. Did your mother come home?"

Polly Pilgrim sounded both polite and happy. "Yes, and I'm at her house now with her," she replied. "I tried to telephone Groucho to tell him the news, but his son answered and said he was out and probably wouldn't be back all afternoon."

"He's tracking down clues, Polly."

The young singer asked, "Are you getting anywhere? What I mean is, do you have any evidence that she's innocent?"

Jane was leaning in the doorway, watching me. I smiled at her. To Polly I said, "We haven't got anything to take to the law yet, but we're finding out quite a bit."

"Like what, Frank?"

"Groucho and I want to talk to your mother—sometime today if possible—and we'll go over everything then, Polly."

"She can't see you today."

"How come?"

"She's not feeling very well, she's sick really."

"You talk to a doctor?"

"Yes, my father sent Dr. Steinberg over. That's our family doctor."

"And he says?"

"Probably influenza, but not a serious case. Though maybe it's food poisoning from the jail meals."

"Okay, tell Frances that Groucho and I will drop in soon as she's feeling up to it," I said. "We'll be seeing you at the Colonel's festivities tonight, won't we?"

"I don't want to go, I'd rather stay with my mother," said Polly forlornly. "My father says, though, that everybody's depending on me to sing tonight. And my mother says if you're a real professional, you go on no matter what's happening offstage. So, yes, I guess I'll be there tonight, Frank."

"Okay, I'll see you at Playland," I said. "Tell your mom we're glad she's out and we're going to see that she stays out."

"Thanks, bye."

I hung up.

Jane asked, "Frances London is free?"

"Right now, yeah. But it could only be a temporary condition."

"You and Groucho have sure found out enough already to convince you she's innocent."

"Convincing Groucho and me isn't exactly the same as convincing cops and lawyers and judges and the district attorney," I pointed out. "But let's get back to my housework. Soon as I finish that, I've got to use the phone to set up interviews with more people."

"Make the calls now," she said. "I'll finish the dishes."

I said, "That's right neighborly of you."

Groucho also did some telephoning that afternoon, installed in one of the phone booths at the back of a Thrifty Drug Store in Pasadena. As he dropped his nickel into the slot, he eyed a young woman in yellow slacks who was bending down to select a love story magazine off the rack a few feet away.

"I prefer an ocean view," he said to himself, "but this is pretty scenic in itself."

"Number, please," requested the operator in a somewhat nasal voice.

Groucho gave her the Maggie Barnes number he'd just bought from her erstwhile agent. "I'd like Ocean fourteen-oh-five, my dear," he said.

The operator said, "There's something very familiar about your voice, sir."

"If you think that's familiar, you ought to see how I behave on the dance floor."

"I know. You must be Groucho Marx."

"Yes, I must," he replied. "It was either that or spend six months in the brig."

"This is certainly a thrill for me, Mr. Marx."

"And for me, too, dear child. Giddy fool that I am, I expected to plop a hard-earned coin into the slot, recite a phone number, and be swiftly put in touch with the person I actually had some desire to talk with," he told her. "But instead, I get to devote untold quantities of precious time to gabbing with a complete and total stranger who—"

"Oh, I'm sorry, Mr. Marx."

"And well you should be, Beulah."

"It's only that I'm such an admirer of your work."

"That's a new one on me. I haven't worked since I left Cripple Creek before the—"

"I meant your work in the movies. I think you and your brothers were wonderful in *A Night at the Opera*. My boyfriend, though, prefers *A Day at the Races*. What do you think?"

"Well now, in my opinion, for what it's worth—and the highest bid thus far has been for three dollars and ninety-six cents—in my humble opinion, let me say without fear of contradiction, or of contraception, for that matter, in my view those two flickers are as different as night and day."

Out in the drug store the girl in the tight slacks was still bent and scanning the love pulps.

"Oh, that's a play on words, isn't it? I mean, *night* is in the title of one of the movies and—"

"Say, did the phone company ever get anywhere with that idea of installing a system whereby a person could stroll into something called a phone booth, insert five cents, and actually get to the party he was desirous of chatting with? It seemed like a simply delightful idea at the time and I can't help wondering if—"

"I'm sorry. I'll put through your call right away, Mr. Marx."

"Thank you, little missy."

"It's been swell talking to you."

"Yes, it has," he agreed. "In fact, my conversation has been so scintillating that *you* ought to pay *me* a nickel."

"I'm ringing Ocean fourteen-oh-five," the operator said, "and getting no answer."

"Give it a few more tries. The young lady in question may just be coming out of a drunken stupor, or a drunken suitor."

"I'm afraid there's still no answer."

Groucho gazed again toward the magazine stand. The pretty girl was gone and a small, extremely freckled boy of about eight was reviewing the latest issue of *Tip Top Comics*. "Were I to mention another phone number, my dear," he said into the mouthpiece, "do you think you could get it for me right away without further discourse?"

"Yes, certainly, Mr. Marx."

"It's not that I don't deeply enjoy intelligent conversations," he assured the operator. "As everyone knows, that's the reason I listen regularly to *Professor Quiz*. However, I'm in a bit of a rush just now and I'm also eager to find out if this phone actually works." He told her the number of Tad Ballard, the trouble-shooter at Paragon Pictures.

Twenty

I wasn't expecting her to answer the door. Far as I knew, Dianne Sayler wasn't even supposed to be at the Brian Montaine mansion on Roxbury Drive in Beverly Hills.

It was a sprawling place in the style real estate people call Early English. There were tall eucalyptus and pepper trees dotting the large emerald lawn. The front door, which looked to have been borrowed from another house, was ornately carved oak.

"You're early," accused Montaine's widow, frowning out at me. She was wearing slacks and a cable-stitch sweater and her face was flushed. "That is if you happen to be Fred Denby."

"Frank Denby. Jane talked to you about my interviewing Edwin Kingsmill, who worked as—"

"Don't I know what Jane talked to me about?" She scrutinized me, slowly, from top to bottom and back to top again. "Well, you're not as dippy looking as I imagined. The way Jane described you, I was expecting a shrimp like Mickey Rooney."

"You should have had her draw you a picture."

Her nose wrinkled. "Another wisenheimer," Dianne observed. "Jane has always had a weakness for lunks with smart mouths."

"Yes, I understand she once had a torrid affair with Albert Einstein. Is Edwin here?"

"Taking a shower. You're early."

"So I've heard."

Dianne sighed. "Hell, you might as well come on in."

I came on in. She led me along a hallway floored with salmon-hued squares of tile and into a beam-ceilinged living room that held too many antique chairs plus a harpsichord.

"You don't want a drink, do you?" inquired the widow, pointing me at a tufted sofa.

"Not especially." From the lavender sofa you could see the swimming pool outside and the row of potted palms on its far side. On the near side of the big turquoise pool a pair of swimming trunks, still damp, was draped over the back of one of the white deck chairs.

"Why does Brian's death interest you anyway? Jane didn't make that especially clear."

"We figure it ties in with Dr. Benninger's death somehow."

She laughed. "This is wonderful," she told me, still laughing. "Here you say *we* and act like you're partners with Perry Mason or the Lone Wolf. When in actuality, you're helping a onetime vaudeville comedian who goes around with a greasepaint moustache."

"Only when he's acting."

"What I'm getting at is—don't you feel stupid being Dr. Watson to Groucho Marx? Is that, after all, a name that commands respect in detective circles?"

"We did okay finding out who murdered Peg McMorrow last fall," I mentioned. "And we're going to find out who's trying to frame Frances London."

"I suppose she's told you she's innocent?"

"Yep, yes."

"I've known quite a few drunks in my life," she said, "and I was married to a dope addict. They're all liars."

"Would you care for a drink, madam?"

"No, Edwin."

I stood and turned.

Edwin Kingsmill was not the typical valet as portrayed on the screen by the likes of Eric Blore and Arthur Treacher. He was a dark and handsome fellow, built along the lines of Gilbert Roland and Cesar Romero."

"You're certain, madam?" He nodded politely at me. "And you, sir?"

"No, thanks. What I'm here for, Kingsmill, is to ask you about—"

"I'd prefer to be addressed as Edwin, sir, if you wouldn't mind."

"Edwin," said Dianne, "I told you about Fred here. He's Jane Danner's boyfriend and he wants to ask you some questions about the night my husband died."

"Your first name is Frank, isn't it, sir?"

"Yeah." I sat down again.

Kingsmill came over and stood with his back to the window and the view of the pool. "How may I help you?" he asked. "Mrs. Montaine has given me permission to discuss the incident with you."

"I think I will have a drink after all." The widow was looking out the window, eyes narrowed slightly.

"At once, madam, if you'll—"

"No, you stay here with Dr. Watson and I'll go fix myself

something." She left the room.

Kingsmill watched her walk away. "Madam, if I may say so, hides her grief behind a mask of flippancy. But inside, I'd venture to say, she's mourning for—"

"Twentieth Century Fox," I said.

"Beg pardon, sir?"

Outside I saw Dianne go dashing over to the damp bathing suit and grab it free of the chair back. Holding it close to her, she ran back toward the house. Kingsmill was unaware of her poolside raid.

"What I meant was, you used to be a player at Twentieth," I told the valet. "I saw you over there a couple of times while I was still working for the *LA Times* and they took me off the police beat to cover show business."

The handsome valet grinned. "I decided I preferred the security of regular employment," he answered. "I haven't been near a sound stage since nineteen thirty-five."

"Perfectly rational decision. Can you tell me about the night you found Brian Montaine's body? And go ahead and sit down."

"I prefer standing, it helps me keep in character."

"What time did you get home?"

"It wasn't until around two in the morning. I had a date over in Pacific Palisades that evening."

"You found him where?"

Kingsmill's eyes looked ceilingward. "Up in the master bedroom. Actually he was spilled out on the floor of the bathroom. He usually injected the stuff in his butt and his trousers were down and the hypo was still sticking in his backside when I found him. He must've given himself too big a dose or it was a bad batch of heroin. I'd guess he died within a few seconds of shooting it into himself, died and fell flat on his face."

I rested my hand on my knee. "Anything to indicate that he might not have given himself that fatal shot?"

"What's that supposed to mean?" I heard the ice in Dianne's glass rattle somewhere behind me.

I kept my attention of the valet. "What I mean is, were there any signs that somebody might have given him the shot?"

The widow came striding into my line of vision. "Are you saying he was murdered?"

"I'm saying he sure as hell might've been."

She glanced at Kingsmill. "You didn't mention anything about his having been—"

"I don't think that's what happened, madam," he answered. Then he frowned. "Of course, there was a bruise on his head." He touched his forefinger to his left temple. "I assumed he was injured when he fell to the tiles."

Dianne moved closer to me. "You think Brian was killed to keep him from making his addiction public?"

"It's not a bad motive for murdering him."

She turned again toward the valet, nearly spilling some of her highball. "Is that possible, Edwin?"

"I suppose it might be, madam."

"Jesus, they could come after me next," she said, dropping into an uncomfortable antique chair. "Brian told me a lot about Jack Cortez and Dr. Benninger." She gulped down half of her scotch highball.

The valet said, "I don't believe they'd deem that necessary."

I asked him, "Before you went out, Edwin, did anyone stop by to see Montaine?"

He shook his head. "No one, sir."

"How about phone calls?"

"There were always phone calls."

147

"Who that particular night?"

"The studio, of course," answered Kingsmill. "As I recall it was one of the Zanksy Brothers—Leon probably. Miss Dubay, the screenwriter, and a reporter from *Screenland*. I'm nearly certain that Dr. Benninger telephoned as well."

"Why didn't you say that right off, nitwit?"

"It only just now occurred to me, madam."

Dianne finished her drink. "I'm sorry I lost my temper."

"Perfectly understandable."

I asked, "Did Montaine take any of the phone calls himself?"

"To the best of my recollection, sir, he spoke to Mr. Zanksy and to the doctor."

"Did he make an appointment to see anyone?"

"That I don't know, sir. When I left here, at a few minutes after eight, no one had been here and Mr. Montaine made no mention of expecting a guest."

"Where was he when you took off?"

He nodded toward the hallway. "In his den, which is at the rear of the house," he said. "A messenger from Paragon had brought over some revised pages of the King Arthur script and he was going over those."

I leaned back in my chair. "Did he have any particular friends—a girlfriend, say—who might just stop by unannounced? Someone who had a key of her own?"

He looked toward the widow. "Well, there was one such person, sir."

She waved her right hand in a loose permissive gesture. "You can go ahead and tell him about that peroxide bitch."

The valet said, "Mr. Montaine had been quite close to a young actress named Karen Ambers. She was playing a lady-in-waiting in *The Legend of King Arthur.*"

148

"That's a laugh," said Dianne, laughing. "That floozie couldn't wait for anything, especially jumping in bed with somebody who could help her career."

"Mr. Montaine hadn't been as close with the young lady in recent weeks, sir," continued Kingsmill. "So it seems unlikely she would have been by that evening. In fact, it's possible that their relationship had already ended."

I nodded. "Okay, now tell me about Tad Ballard and what he did after you called him," I requested.

The Paragon Pictures studios lay in the middle of Culver City, covered about thirty acres, and were surrounded by a high freshly painted plank fence. There was a billboard-size poster touting *The Legend of King Arthur* stretching along the planks to the left of the studio gates.

The heavyset guard used to work at MGM and he smiled at Groucho. "I hear you and the boys finally got a job again," he remarked as Groucho pulled his Cadillac up to the guard shack.

"Yes, Michael, we're working as stand-ins for the Boswell Sisters," answered Groucho. "I get to double Connie, which is just oodles of fun."

Chuckling, the hefty guard studied the visitor roster. "Julius Marx. Guess that's you. You have an appointment to see Tad Ballard at two-thirty." He grimaced. "Why do you want to see that jerk?"

"Purely in the line of duty."

"Seriously now, Groucho, what's the name of your new movie?"

"Seriously, Michael, it's not a movie but an animated cartoon. It'll be in Disney's *Silly Symphonies* series and I'm set to play the leading buttercup," explained Groucho. "Originally I was slated to be Goofy, but my reading of 'Gorsh,' was considered inadequate and the part went to Ronald Colman instead."

"It's impossible to get a straight answer out of you."

"If I started giving out straight answers, my boy, I'd be even less employable than I am now."

"Go on in, Groucho, and park in Lot A. You'll find the jerk in Office Building Two."

"Thank you and give my best to the little ones."

"I don't have any kids, Groucho."

"I heard you were romancing a couple of midgets. Adieu."

He drove on into the studio grounds, coming to a stop so that a platoon of Foreign Legionnaires could march across the street.

"Imagine all those fellows trying to forget."

Lot A was crowded and it took him nearly five minutes to find an empty slot. Lighting a fresh cigar, Groucho went loping along a curving street lined with stately palm trees.

Office Building 2 was a two-story structure with red tile roofs and a peach-colored stucco façade.

After pausing to ogle a starlet who went whizzing by on a boy's bicycle, Groucho slouched up the red tile steps and popped into the reception area.

The plump young receptionist behind the wide curved desk sat up and exclaimed, "Groucho Marx."

"Everybody has been saying that to me today." He skulked closer to her desk. "What does it mean, my dear? Is it some Gypsy curse, the first line of the Albanian national anthem, the lyric of a new Tony Pastor novelty tune?"

"It's your name."

"Ah, how disappointing, just another meaningless phrase

then." He exhaled smoke. "I'm Otto von Bismarck, dear child, and I have an appointment with Tad Ballard."

Her plump face took on an unhappy expression. "Oh, gee."

"Really?"

"What I mean is that Mr. Ballard isn't here."

"Elsewhere, is he?"

"Yes, he's over on Sound Stage Five, which is where they were shooting the interiors for *The Legend of King Arthur* before poor Brian Montaine kicked the bucket," she said. "He had to rush over to help out the new publicity girl who suddenly felt she wasn't up to showing a bunch of newspaper people around and explaining to them how Paragon is going to finish the movie as a tribute to Brian Montaine. Well, that part she could handle, but not lying about how they're hoping they can use his stand-in to film the twenty percent of the darn thing that's not done yet. So that's where Mr. Ballard is."

"I don't suppose Ballard would mind if I wandered over there and kibitzed until he was finished and free to chat with me."

She shrugged. "So long as you don't clown around and screw up their pitch to the newspaper idiots."

Groucho leaned an elbow on her desk and gazed deeply into her eyes. "You have no doubt heard, my sweet, that inside every clown there is a serious person?"

"I've heard that, yes."

"Well, I just had my serious person surgically removed and I'm liable to behave like an absolute buffoon."

"Actually, that's okay by me, Mr. Marx."

"With your kind permission then, I will take my leave." He grabbed up her pudgy left hand and gave it a smacking kiss. "I may not come back from the front, Renee, so this is farewell. At this point, if you must know, I'm even having trouble telling the front from the back except that I think the back has a pleat in it." He kissed her hand once more and then went trotting out into the afternoon.

Twenty-one

There was a suckling pig, an apple in its mouth, sprawled on a silver platter at the center of the Round Table. Seated around the massive table, in ornate high-backed oaken chairs, were five people who were probably reporters, a very nervous blond young woman and Tad Ballard. Ballard was in his late thirties, tan, with an Errol Flynn sort of moustache.

As Groucho watched, partly concealed by a canvas flat that represented a portion of castle wall, the studio troubleshooter lit his cork-tipped cigarette with a glittering gold lighter and chuckled.

"What Esther meant to say, folks, is that Paragon won't be conning the American public in any way," he told them. "Fortunately, at the time of Brian's unfortunate and untimely death, *The Legend of King Arthur* was close to ninety-five percent completed." He flicked ashes in the direction of the plaster prop pig. "What you and Brian's millions of fans will eventually see on the screen, when this latest Paragon Pictures epic is released—very close to schedule, I might add—what you'll see, folks, will be nobody but the late Brian Montaine in the role of his lifetime, the legendary King Arthur."

"No doubles? No back shots of a look-alike?" asked the fat reporter from the *Herald-Examiner*. "That's not the way I heard it, Tad."

"Sometimes, so I hear, your hearing ain't so good, Mark." Ballard ground out his cigarette by sweeping it across the underside of the table. "Okay, folks, I have another meeting to hit. Thanks for your time and now, for them as wants to, Esther will take you on a tour of the outdoor King Arthur sets. I think you're going to be especially impressed by the jousting field. It's authentic as all get-out. Esther, honey."

The blond young woman pushed back in her heavy oaken chair. "If," she said, clearing her throat, "if you'll all tag along with me, we'll go do that."

Ballard watched them trail her off the set. "I hope," he called, "you'll all help us make this a fitting tribute to the memory one of Hollywood's great talents, the late Brian Montaine."

Groucho stepped out from behind the canvas wall and went striding across the castle floor. "Give me a moment to control my tears, Tad," he requested. "Then we can have our postponed meeting."

"Groucho, hi." Ballard looked at his silver wristwatch. "You have to keep in mind that Hollywood is built on a firm foundation of bullshit."

"Yes, and you're one of its most distinguished architects."

The troubleshooter consulted the watch again. "I actually am running way behind today, Groucho." He rested his backside against the edge of the Round Table. "You were sort of vague on the telephone, but I agreed to fit you in. Hell, we're friends from way back and—"

"You've already spread enough foundation for one day, Tad," suggested Groucho. He hoisted himself up and sat on the table.

"I came to chat about Brian Montaine."

"A marvelous actor. It's a damn shame he had that heart attack . . ." He lowered his head, shaking it sadly. "Hell of a nice guy, too."

Groucho tilted slightly forward and turned his head toward Ballard. "But he didn't have a heart attack," he said. "He died from an overdose of heroin and you covered the whole thing up."

Ballard stiffened, sliding off the table. He spun, glaring at Groucho. "Where do you get off accusing me of—"

"We have witnesses, my boy," Groucho told him quietly. "Now I can trot over to that famous jousting field and mention their names to your reporter chums—or we can have a private talk here with only the pig as witness."

"I don't know what the hell you're talking about. And if—"

Groucho dropped free of the Round Table. "Why don't I catch up with Mark Evans from the *Herald-Examiner*? He's not an especial fan of yours and—"

"Okay, hold it." He took hold of Groucho's arm. "Why are you interested in any of this?"

"Because it connects with Frances London's troubles."

"That lush? Why do you give a damn about—"

"Humor me, Tad. Write it off to an old man's whim—but tell me about your cover-up." He pulled free of the trouble-shooter's grip.

"Shit." Ballard sat again in the ornate chair he'd occupied earlier. "All right. What do you want to know?"

"Just about everything," Groucho told him.

* * *

As I shaved, I scrutinized myself in Jane's bathroom mirror. "You didn't really tell Dianne Sayler I was dippy looking, did you?"

"What?" she called from the living room.

I left the bathroom, crossed the bedroom and looked into the living room.

Jane was sitting in an armchair, long legs crossed, going over some proof sheets of the *Hillbilly Willie* comic strip. "What were you bellowing about?"

"Dippy. Did you mention to your old art school chum that I was somewhat dippy?"

Smiling, she lowered the proofs to her lap and shook her head. 'Now, see? That's exactly how rumors get started," she said. "I told her you were *sappy* and, by the time it got back to you, the message was all distorted."

"Okay, *sappy* I can accept. How about my being a shrimp?"

"I only mentioned that you weren't tall."

"Five foot nine isn't exactly short."

"But you're only five nine if you walk around on tiptoe, Frank. I figured she might catch you by surprise sometime and notice that you were really only five eight and think—"

"I'm going to have to hire my own press agent to counter all this negative propaganda that's floating around."

Jane said, "I've been thinking about what you said about Dianne and the valet."

"And?"

After setting the proofs on the rug, she stood up and stretched. "Well, if she has been having an affair with that guy— could they maybe have murdered Brian Montaine?"

I ran a knuckle over my chin, getting foam all over my thumb. "There is, I suppose, a motive," I conceded. "Classic one, in fact. Handsome servant helps restless wife knock off spouse. They then share in fortune she inherits. Good James M. Cain sort of plot."

"It is, I admit, trite."

"Problem there would be," I added, "that if they murdered Montaine for his money—well, then his death doesn't connect with the killing of Dr. Benninger. And that's the murder we really have to solve."

"Suppose Benninger slipped them the stuff they used to kill Brian."

"So?"

"We know the doctor had money problems," said Jane. "He goes back to them and demands a larger fee than they'd agreed on. Otherwise he'll sing."

"You been reading *Dames Love Diamonds*? Sing?"

"If they don't give him more money, he'll reveal the true circumstances of Brian Montaine's demise."

I shook my head. "He couldn't threaten that. Benninger, if we accept your scenario, is an accessory. He couldn't turn them in without screwing himself, too."

"But you and Groucho believe he did have something to do with Brian's death."

"Sure, but not in cahoots with the widow and that gigolo."

Bending, Jane gathered up the proofs and took a few steps in the direction of her studio. "If you don't value my suggestions, you can simply say so and I won't—"

"I value your suggestions, Jane. I value you," I assured her. "I don't, however, feel like I have to accept every blessed idea that falls from your lips or—"

"You can try making your points without shouting."

"I wasn't shouting. Had I been shouting, Jane, several of the lightbulbs would've popped and a window pane or two."

"*Now* you are being dippy." She left the living room.

I went back and finished shaving for the Colonel's party.

Twenty-two

Most nights the big tent pitched at the center of the King Neptune Playland at the Beach was the home of a girlie show called Honolulu Honeys. Tonight, since Colonel Mullens had hired the entire amusement park for his birthday party, the tent was going to be used for the entertainment that included Groucho and Polly.

The wind that had come up at sundown was worrying the canvas sides of the tent, causing them to shake and produce occasional popping sounds. About two hundred folding chairs were arranged in rows on the sawdust-covered plank floor. The whole place smelled of stale beer, perspiration, and something that was either cheap perfume or insect spray.

There was a small elevated stage up at the front of the tent with five chairs and a piano on the floor right below it.

No one was in the tent. I stood just inside the entrance for a few minutes, taking it all in. Then I made my way down the center sawdust aisle. The spangled curtain, which had a fading painting of hula dancers on a tropical beach decorating it, was partially open.

Walking up the six wooden steps at the side of the platform,

I reached the stage. Now I could see a plywood partition at the back. It had an unpainted door at its center and lettered in white-wash, in an arbitrary mix of uppercase and lowercase letters, were the words dRessiNg rOomS.

"Not quite the Palace," I said.

"When do the elephants arrive?"

Groucho, carrying his guitar case, his makeup kit and a large paper-wrapped bundle, was loping along the aisle toward the stage.

Outside in the windy dusk the merry-go-round started up, playing a pipe organ version of "Happy Days Are Here Again."

Dropping everything, Groucho straightened up and saluted. After a few seconds he said, "Ah, forgive me. I thought they were playing the national anthem." Taking out a cigar, he glanced around the tent. "Where's my amazingly cute little co-star?"

"Not here yet," I answered. "Nobody is."

"I assume they've shooed the chimpanzees out of my dressing room and I can unload my wandering minstrel equipment someplace hereabouts?"

Returning down to the sawdust, I reached for his bundle. "Dressing rooms are behind that partition yonder."

"Take it up tenderly," he cautioned me, gathering up his guitar and the makeup box. "I've got Nelson Eddy's hat in there and I intend to wear it for my duet with Pollyanna."

"Which hat?" I went climbing up the steps again.

"The one he sported in *Rosemarie.* My brother Chico knows a girl—well, no, actually, Chico knows, at last count, two thousand and three girls. This particular one, however, has access to the MGM wardrobe facilities and she was able to extract the actual skimmer Eddy wore while yodeling to Jeanette MacDonald and pretending to be a Royal Canadian Mountie. Of course, if he were half a man, he'd have doffed the hat and mounted the lady, but—"

"That would've capsized the canoe." I lugged the bundle to the partition. The door made a rusty sound when I yanked it open.

"Speaking of Chico, also known as the Oversexed Rover Boy, he passed along an interesting fact about Polly's pop."

We found seven cubbyholes behind the partition, each one with an old army blanket on a wire serving as a door. Pinned on the second blanket from the left was a sheet of tablet paper with *Marx* scrawled on it in purple ink.

Groucho wandered along inspecting the labels on the other blankets. "Aha," he said at the fourth blanket. "Rita Hayworth. A very impressive young lady and a spiffy dancer. Can't act at all, but it little matters. I first encountered her back when she was calling herself Margarita Cansino but her father discouraged me from paying attention to her. And, when a fellow uses a knife about this long to discourage me, I tend to get discouraged and—"

"What about Pilgrim?"

Drawing aside the blanket that guarded the entry to his cubbyhole, Groucho peered in. There was a rickety makeup table with a streaked mirror attached, a folding metal chair, and a hat rack with a brass eagle atop it. The light was provided by a dangling 60-watt bulb.

"Damme, sirrah," he remarked, "I had better quarters at MGM and Louis B. Mayer loathes me." Entering, he placed the guitar case on the plank floor and rested the makeup kit on the table. "In fact, I had a better dressing room when we played the

Black Hole of Calcutta. And it smelled a great deal more fragrant."

"Something about Polly's father?" I reminded.

"Like my dear scatterbrained brother, it seems Old Man Pilgrim has a fondness for games of chance and betting on sporting contests." Groucho gazed up at the shadowy canvas top of the tent far above. "Are those bats I see dangling up there?"

"And?"

"The gent is deeply in hock, so rumor has it."

"C'mon, Groucho, he comes from a family that's been wealthy for generations here in California." When I set the bundle on the chair, the chair teetered and started to topple to the left. I caught it, got it righted and balanced. "His public relations outfit takes in all kinds of dough promoting right-wing politicians and their causes. And he must skim a goodly chunk off Polly's money."

"Nevertheless." Groucho was staring at himself in the mirror. "Have I developed freckles or is this thing flyspecked?"

"You're suggesting that Pilgrim owes money to people like Vince Salermo and similar hoodlums and gamblers?"

"According to the ever reliable Chico, he owes a pretty penny."

"Then he must be especially anxious to make sure Polly signs that contract with Paragon."

"Exactly, Rollo," he said, licking the tip of his forefinger and rubbing at the surface of the glass. "By the bye, my beloved sibling also informed me, when I mentioned the site of tonight's little fiasco, that there's something called the Filmland Wax Museum on the premises."

"Yeah, over beyond the Fun House. I noticed it coming in."

"There is supposedly a tableau of myself and three of my

cherubic brothers on display there for all the world to see."

"And you want to see it?"

"So few artists have ever been able to capture my true innate beauty," he explained, "that I live in the constant hope that someone will finally succeed. Do you want to go take a gander before I have to start rehearsing?"

"Sure, okay," I agreed. "What did you find out about the girl who slipped you the death threat?"

"Her name is Maggie Barnes."

"An actress?"

Taking my arm, Groucho led me out of his cubicle. "This may break your heart, Merton, but I fear the lady has fallen on hard times," he told me. "When she's not working as a gun moll, she apparently puts in time at a local bawdy house."

"Have you talked to her yet?"

Slouching along the sawdust aisle, he answered, "No, since she hasn't been home all the livelong day. In a mood to sacrifice, I intend to call on her at her place of business after tonight's festivities."

"Hey, that isn't safe."

"I don't intend to avail myself of her carnal services, Rollo, only talk with dear Maggie."

"Every whore house in LA is owned and operated by gangsters," I reminded him. "Suppose they find out that you're there?"

"You're unlikely to find them underfoot. They're usually lolling around their mansions in Bel Air or Malibu, my lad," he assured me. "I shall simply pop in, convince the lass she should tell all, and then take my leave. I won't even hug her, I'll eschew a farewell address."

"Even so, Groucho, you—"

"Of course, if the eschew is on the other foot, there's no telling what could transpire."

"I think you ought to wait and see her at home."

"Should I have said something about taking a plug of eschewing tobacco along?"

"No."

We were outside now and the amusement park was starting to come to life. Few guests had arrived, but more and more colored lights were blossoming across the darkening sky, neon signs were starting to blink and flash, several kinds of loud music were pouring out of speakers.

"While we're en route to this temple of the arts," suggested Groucho, "we can compare notes. I was intending to entitle my report on my activities *My Day,* but it turns out Eleanor Roosevelt beat me to the title."

"I think you've mentioned that to me before."

"Brilliant remarks, let me remind you, can certainly bear repeating," he pointed out. "Take that 'To be or not to be' routine. You've heard that more than once, I'll wager."

Rising up in front of the brightly painted Fun House was a huge automated clown inside a glass cage. He was wearing a silky crimson costume, had a white goggle-eyed face dominated by a red bulb of a nose. "Ho ho ho," he said. "Ho ho ho."

"Let's make sure that chap gets a front-row seat for the show," said Groucho.

There was no ticket taker on duty at the Filmland Wax Museum. Tacked to the front of the ticket booth was a hand-lettered sign announcing, FREE TONIGHT!

Gingerbread trim painted blue, red, and gold framed the entrance and a cloth banner strung above the doorway promised

LIFELIKE, LIFE-SIZE REPLICAS OF THE GREATS OF FILM-LAND!

Groucho and I entered. The place apparently consisted of a linked series of small display rooms and we had the initial one to ourselves. It was chill, musty. Set up around the room on low wooden pedestals were wax effigies of Charlie Chaplin, Harold Lloyd, Buster Keaton, Laurel and Hardy, W. C. Fields, Bob Hope, and a skinny fellow I didn't recognize. Most of the likenesses weren't bad, although the comedians all had the complexions of painted dolls.

"Explain to me why I'm not in this room." He gestured at the array of figures. "It's obviously devoted chiefly to great comedians."

"Maybe the great comedians who are members of family groups have a separate room."

Hands behind his back, Groucho went shuffling over to study the statue of Bob Hope. "Upstart," he muttered. "Judging by what you learned from the valet, Rollo, and what I persuaded Tad Ballard of Paragon Pictures to confide, we can pretty much conclude that Brian Montaine was murdered and that Dr. Benninger played a part in the killing."

"We can't prove Montaine was murdered," I said. "And after the funeral, as Jane told us, they cremated the guy."

"Sifting that hambone's ashes won't establish he was bopped on the coco before being giving a lethal shot in the tochis." He sighed, turning his back on Hope. "Imagine spending all eternity with no backside." He drifted toward the doorway to the next chamber. "What do you think of Janey's theory?"

"That Dianne and the valet teamed up to bump Montaine off?" I followed him. "I suppose it's possible, but I don't believe he was killed so somebody could inherit his money."

"Silencing him seems the more likely motive. Ah, here's Joan Crawford."

A dozen wax figures of movie actresses circled this room. Joan Crawford, in her Sadie Thompson costume, was sitting in a chair on the platform to the right of the entrance.

"Did I ever tell you about what transpired between Joan and myself in that phone booth in Tijuana?"

"You did, yes sir."

"Would you like me to retell it?"

"Nope."

"Perhaps I'll write it up and sell it to the *Reader's Digest*." He moved further into the room. "The Most Unforgettable Character I Ever Shared a Phone Booth With."

"Snappy title."

"I'll be jiggered. They've got Louise Brooks on display." He was gazing up at the wax figure of the dark-haired actress. "Takes me back to my youth—and that's starting to be an all-day trip. I had an enormous yen for her in the early twenties."

"What happened?"

Eyebrows climbing, he looked at me briefly over his shoulder. "You refuse to hear a recounting of my tender telephonic interlude with Miss Crawford, you young reprobate, but the possibility that I diddled a madcap *Follies* girl excites your lewd libido?"

"That must be it, yes."

"I was going to digress and make a few well-chosen remarks about Ida Libido, but I shall refrain," he decided. "As a matter of fact, Dr. Adler, I believe I am the one and only Broadway playboy who didn't carry on with Louise. It has all the ingredients of a romantic tragedy, though I'll be the first to admit that *Groucho and Louise* doesn't have quite the zing of *Romeo and Juliet*."

Shaking his head sadly, Groucho loped into the next room.

"Eureka," I heard him exclaim.

The Marx Brothers figures were there, standing side by side with arms linked. Except for Harpo, who had his knee being held up by Groucho. Chico was there along with Zeppo.

As he shuffled around the platform, Groucho observed, "Gad, Zeppo hasn't looked this good in years. He really should come here and have his puss waxed by these people." When he halted before his own image, a scowl appeared on his face. "I, on the other hand, look like Rasputin on a bad day."

He rose up on tiptoe, stretching to flick a speck of lint off the frock coat of the wax Groucho.

Behind us I heard a leather shoe sole rasp on wood and a metallic click.

"Look out." I dived forward and tackled Groucho.

We both went slamming into the floor and up above us the head of the Groucho figure exploded when the bullet hit it.

Twenty-three

The second bullet went thunking into the floor about six inches from where the real Groucho's head had been seconds earlier.

He'd gone rolling across the floor, then scurried behind the platform that held what was left of the wax Marx Brothers.

Myself, I'd rolled, too, bumping against the platform and causing Harpo's hat and wig to go flying free of his head.

Just as I ducked down beside Groucho, a third slug hit Zeppo in the knee and sent fragments of cloth and wax raining down on us.

The wax figure lurched, swayed and fell over backward off the planks. Zeppo dropped down on us both, his right hand giving me a waxy smack in the eye.

The manikin rolled free, slammed into the floor behind us, and one of his glass eyes popped free of its socket.

There was no more shooting and an immense silence seemed to close in on us.

Then I heard footsteps running away.

All I'd ever seen of the gunmen was part of his right arm thrust through the doorway, a gun, a gloved hand, and a dark blue coat sleeve.

"Are you bullet-ridden, Rollo?" Grunting and scrambling, Groucho got himself into an awkward sitting position.

"No. How about you?"

He shook his head, shedding flecks of wax. "I'm still as sound as a dollar," he said. "Make that sound as two-bit piece."

I figured it was safe to rise. On my feet, I extended a hand to help Groucho get up. "Think that was a real attempt to kill us?" I asked him. "Or only one more try to scare us?"

After frowning at the sprawled wax replica of his fallen brother, Groucho answered, "I don't know about you, Eloise, but I was sufficiently scared already. Still and all, if they'd been trying for a serious assassination, they would probably have sent someone who was a better shot."

Bending, I gathered up the battered Harpo hat and curly red wig. "You and Zeppo sustained the most damage."

"It was that way around the house when we were youths, too." He squatted, poked at the remains of his waxen head. He picked up the nose, turned it around in his hand. "No wonder I've been drummed out of the lonely hearts club. What rational woman could love a shnoz like this?"

"When did you start going in for rational women?"

"People who live with cartoonists shouldn't throw stones," he advised. "Though if you want to throw a scone on occasion, that might be allowed. It would depend, of course, on the occasion. For example, National Scone Throwing Day might be suitable. However, if—"

"We're going to have to report this to somebody."

Groucho dropped the wax nose into his jacket pocket and left the room. "All in good time, Renfrew," he said as I followed him through the room where the images of the movie actresses were. "I don't imagine the management of this vast illuminated flea market is going to be too very upset about losing a few carven images of the Marx Clan." He paused to give Joan Crawford a friendly pat on the backside and then continued toward the way out. "Now, had it been the Three Stooges or—"

"As I recall, though, Emily Post tells us it's bad manners not to report an attempt on one's life."

"Shooting a wax dummy isn't a crime, is it?" He increased his pace as we neared the final exit.

"Even so, I think . . . Well, good evening, Sergeant Branner."

The Bayside police detective was leaning against the wax museum ticket booth. He wasn't wearing gloves, but his suit was a dark blue.

"Is this indeed our favorite most minion of the law, the flatfoot's flatfoot Sergeant Branner?" Groucho produced a fresh cigar and unwrapped it. "You're certain it's not another of those clever wax dummies?"

"Am I wrong," asked Branner, smiling thinly, "or did I hear some shooting just now?"

"Somebody took a few shots at us." I pointed back toward the museum. "In there, which you probably already know about."

"I was thinking about going in and investigating," the lanky cop told us. "In fact, I'll have a look right now. Did *you* shoot anybody?"

"No, we were the targets."

He reached out and took the book of matches from Groucho's hand. "Mind if I borrow a light?" After lighting his cigarette, he continued. "Either of you see the guy who did the shooting?"

"No, only part of his arm sticking through the doorway," I answered. "Looked like a .38 Police Special. His suit was the same color as yours."

"It's a very fashionable shade this season," said the detective, taking a deep drag on his cigarette. "Tell you what. I'll give the museum the once-over, see what I can turn up. Considering that Colonel Mullens wouldn't like a full-scale police investigation interrupting his big bash here, I'll keep the lid on this for now."

Groucho lit his cigar. "That is, surprisingly, an excellent idea, sergeant."

Branner tapped me on the chest with the hand that held the cigarette. That got ashes on my tie. "This incident, Denby, is a good example of what happens to saps who get the idea they're detectives. Think about that."

"You might think about it, too."

Groucho tugged on my sleeve and got me headed back toward the tent.

The Mullens Maidens sidetracked us.

Or rather, they sidetracked Groucho. I just hung around to make certain he got safely back to the entertainment tent.

There were a half dozen of them, all dressed in low-fronted, short-skirted costumes that made them resemble wholesome cigarette girls. Each one carried a wicker basket full up with the yellow and blue cardboard packages of Mullens Pudding. All five flavorful flavors were available to the Colonel's impending guests.

Five of the Maidens were gathered in front of a kiosk that had been set up on the amusement park grounds. It was labeled MULLENS PUDDING PAVILION. A smaller sign invited guests to MEET THE MULLENS MAIDENS AND GET YOUR FREE BOX OF DELIGHTFULLY DELICIOUS MULLENS PUDDING!

The sixth girl had set down her gift basket and climbed up a stepladder that was leaning against the kiosk. She was struggling to post a sign that said HAPPY BIRTHDAY, COLONEL MULLENS!

She was a redhead and when Groucho noted her having trouble with her tack hammer, he came to a stop. "Here's a damsel in distress, Sancho, or I miss my guess," he announced. "And, since I've already missed my bus, there's time to tarry and offer her assistance. There might even be time for *Terry and the Pirates.*"

"By now Polly's probably at the tent," I mentioned. "If you intend to impersonate Nelson Eddy, you ought to—"

"Spontaneity has always been the key to my performances." He flicked ashes from his cigar and started trotting in the direction of the redhead on the ladder. "And the Rosetta Stone has always been the key to deciphering my after-dinner speeches."

After I took a couple of deep breaths in and out, I walked over to the Pudding Pavilion.

"Pudding, sir? It's absolutely free." One of the Mullens Maidens had stepped into my path, preventing me from continuing in Groucho's wake. She was a slim blond girl of about twenty and the chill night wind coming in off the Pacific was causing goose bumps on her bare arms and legs.

"I'm Frank Denby," I told her. "I work on the show and get all the free pudding I can use."

"Oh, you're the writer, aren't you? What I mean is, you turn out the scripts for *Groucho Marx, Private Eye.*"

I nodded, somewhat surprised. "Most people don't recognize my—"

"My name is Victoria St. John. Well, actually it's not exactly that because Victoria St. John is my stage and screen name, even though I haven't as yet appeared on either but it's a lot more interesting sounding, at least I think so, than my real name of Victoria Winiarsky," she said. "I intend, which is the point I'm leading up to, and I mention that because I can see that look in your eye that people get when they think I'm just rambling on in some kind of stream of conscience Joycean way and don't realize I'm heading for a logical conclusion, even though I have this tendency to digress, which I'm certain you've noticed, the point is that I want to succeed in show business, but not in the usual obvious way, even though I'm a fairly attractive girl and I don't see why I shouldn't be honest about that, by having to let all the oafs who are in influential positions in the movie industry paw me just so I can get a two-day bit part in some B-movie about a bunch of halfwits in tuxedos shooting at each other and turning nice girls into saloon hostesses and that's why I pay attention to what's going on."

I looked at her thoughtfully. "Was the reason you recognize me in that monologue someplace?"

Groucho was now sharing the ladder with the red-haired young woman, helping her to tack up the birthday greeting poster.

Victoria said, "It's my goal to succeed in the acting field and as soon as I got this job, which I've been at nearly three weeks now, I decided I had to find out as much about what was going on as I could if I didn't want to spend my life being a Mullens Maiden and standing around in a skimpy costume like this and freezing my extremities and so I wangled myself tickets for *Groucho Marx, Private Eye* and I saw the broadcast week before last and I made sure I memorized the names of all the actors and the announcer and the director and the writer. When you stood up and took a bow, after Harry Whitechurch introduced you before it went on the air, I made a mental note to remember your name along with all the rest."

"You're aiming for the movies, huh?"

"For now, but eventually I don't see any reason why I can't

eventually go on the stage, too."

I took another glance at Groucho. He was still up on the ladder with the redhead. "Could you talk like this if you were reading from a radio script?" I asked the blond girl.

"Talk like what, Mr. Denby?"

"In this bubbly voice and with all the circumlocutions, Victoria."

"I don't think, and please, don't get the idea that I'm bragging or have a swell head, but I pretty much always talk like this, even though a lot of my friends, and especially my relatives, often suggest I pipe down, and so I really don't see why it would be a problem to act in the same style if that's what you're curious about."

"Okay, tell me where I can get in touch with you. I think maybe—"

"Oh, gosh, is this just going to be one of those situations where you pretend you can get me into the movies if only I'm cooperative and where cooperative means taking off my clothes and things like that, because it struck me, even when I just saw you from the fifth row, which wasn't a bad seat when you consider that I got my ticket a the last minute almost, that you were a decent-seeming fellow?"

"I absolutely can't get you in the movies," I assured Victoria. "And I'm already spoken for and that's a situation that looks to last for the next few decades. But the actress who's been playing Groucho's secretary on the show is quitting to go do a soap opera in Chicago and I'm thinking that if we're going to get a new actress, we might also try a new secretary. One who talks somewhat like you do, Victoria." I took out one of my business cards. "If you'll feel safer about this, you phone me. In a couple days, okay?"

175

She smiled, accepted the card and tucked it away between her breasts.

"Now this is the sort of thing I like to see with all my many employees. The lowest, the highest and all those in between. They're friendly with each other, they share the joys and sorrows of working for Mullens Pudding," said a deep chesty voice behind me. "All of us are, after all, on the same darn team, aren't we? From a humble Mullens Maiden to a high-paid scriptwriter. Good evening, Frank, and how are you?"

I turned to see big wide Colonel Mullens, abundant white hair flickering in the night wind, smiling paternally at me. I didn't contradict the high-paid remark, instead smiling falsely and saying, "Happy birthday, Colonel."

He shook my hand, eyes on Victoria. "And you, my dear, are who?"

"Victoria St. John, Colonel Mullens. We met at the grand opening of that new grocery market in Altadena week before last."

"Yes, we did, Victoria."

The Colonel's son, a large blond young man in his late twenties, and two very well dressed men who were no doubt from the Manhattan ad agency were flanking the pudding tycoon.

The Colonel asked me, "You know my youngest son, Collin, don't you, Frank?"

"Hi, Collin." We shook hands.

"These two fellows are Buzz Hodges, the Mullens account executive, and Jack Rolphs, the associate account exec. Just in from New York for my birthday."

I shook hands with the pair of them.

Collin nodded in my direction, saying, "This is as good a time as any to tell him, Dad."

"Not on my birthday, son."

"What? Tell me what?" I looked from father to son and back to father.

Hodges, who was taller than his colleague and had very short-cropped graying hair, said, "You might as well be made aware that the ratings on *Groucho Marx, Private Eye* have been slipping seriously, Frank."

"When we introduce the new flavor in June," added Rolphs, "we need your little show to have a much larger audience than it commands now."

"New flavor?"

Groucho, I noticed, was climbing down the ladder.

"There's a new flavor coming in June, just in time for all the newlywed brides to try," explained Colonel Mullens. "Raspberry."

"But if you have six flavors, it'll spoil the alliteration," I told them.

Rolphs said, "You'll be getting a copy of my memos pertaining to ways to improve the show in the mail within the next day or so, Frank."

"Improve it?" I realized that I seemed to be doing nothing much but asking short questions.

Collin Mullens shifted his feet, made an impatient noise. "I guess I'm going to have to tell him," he said.

Putting his hand on his son's arm, the Colonel said, smiling broadly, "My youngest boy here is something of a writer himself, Frank. While he was at USC Collin always got excellent grades in English composition and he also wrote the skits for the Phi Sig Homecoming Dance three years running."

"Wait now," I said. "You're trying to tell me that Collin is going to take over the scripting?"

"Hey, it isn't that at all," Collin assured me. "What I'm going to be is a consultant. You go on writing your scripts same as always. Well, not exactly the same, since you'll have to change things to accommodate the swell suggestions Jack and Buzz will be sending you. Anyway, all I'm going to do is polish your stuff, Frank."

"Polish it? A guy who's sole writing credit is for fraternity skits?"

"Might I join this powwow?" Groucho came slouching up.

"Groucho, how wonderful." Colonel Mullens brightened, chuckling and holding out his hand. "It's great seeing you again. You know my youngest son, Collin, and these two handsome fellows are from the New York advertising agency that does such a great job handling our—"

"Ah, you are exactly the people I want most to see." He ignored the Colonel's proffered hand. "Which one of you is Batten and which one is Down-the-Hatches?"

"My name," said Rolphs evenly, "is Jack Rolphs and my associate is Buzz Hodges."

Groucho's cigar had gone out and he paused now to light it. "I couldn't help overhearing some of your spirited conversation with *my* associate," he said, puffing on the cigar. "And it inspired me to come up with what I think is a brilliant new title for the radio show." The smoke he exhaled went swirling away on the wind. "Let's call it *Collin Mullens, Private Eye.*"

The Colonel frowned. "I'm afraid, Groucho, the point you're trying to make doesn't—"

"Do you have to use spectacles for reading? I know I have to."

"My eyesight is fine. But what—"

"I suggest you read again the contract you signed with me,

Colonel," said Groucho. "Therein, as those of us well versed in legal jargon are wont to say, you'll read a clause that I had my own team of overpriced shysters insert. It reads, and this, mind you, is a rough paraphrase, it reads—'Groucho Marx, hereinafter to be known as the Party of The Second Part and sometimes, especially when there's a full moon, as the Singing Sheriff of Old Cheyenne, has complete and total script approval and control over who shall and who shall not write the damn things.' " He blew out smoke. "In layman's terms—which were, as you all know, first used by Abe Layman in 1913—I am the one who says who writes my show. Not you, dear Colonel, or your son or city slickers from the East. If you'd like me to exit the show right here and now, then go ahead with your plans to have someone other than Frank work on the scripts."

For about five seconds at least there followed what you might call a stunned silence.

Then the Colonel cleared his throat. "As a performer, Groucho, you have a reputation for being outspoken," he said slowly, anger in his voice. "Let me remind you, however, that I won't be addressed in this manner by any of my employees or told—"

"Do you want me out of the show?" asked Groucho. "If so, I'll pick up my guitar and head for home to phone my attorneys. On the other hand, should you come to your senses, we'll continue with the festivities as planned."

Up above to the right the giant roller-coaster had just been lit up. I can't ride those things without having a vertigo attack, but I felt now as though I'd been rattling along in one for the past ten minutes or so.

Rolphs had been whispering in Hodges's ear. He said finally, "We're willing to give you four more weeks to bring up the ratings, Groucho. Provided you and Frank make an honest effort to take our suggestions for improvement of *Groucho Marx, Private Eye* into consideration. After that, and depending on the ratings, we'll reevaluate the situation."

The Colonel said, "I don't know."

"I can wait four weeks, Dad," said his son, not looking directly at me.

"Very well," said Colonel Mullens. "I'll go along with you on this, Groucho. After all, there are several hundred people who came here tonight to see you."

Saying nothing, Groucho started off for the entertainment tent.

The Colonel, his son, and the advertising men grunted and nodded at me and left.

I stood there, watching the bright-lit roller-coaster cars go through a swooping test run.

"Do you still want me to call you?" Victoria had been standing nearby throughout the impromptu outdoor conference.

"That depends," I told her, "on how you feel about traveling on sinking ships."

She smiled. "Sounds like fun to me," she said.

Twenty-four

Polly Pilgrim asked me, "How many more encores is he likely to take?"

"When Groucho reaches the Gilbert and Sullivan phase," I told her, "there's really no way of telling."

Out on the tent stage Groucho had followed his encore medley of selections from *The Mikado* with a medley of selections from *The Pirates of Penzance*. That had all come after the selection of tunes from the Marx Brothers' movies.

He was the movie-Groucho now. He'd painted on his moustache and enhanced his eyebrows, slipped into the rumpled frock coat and the baggy pants he'd brought in his bundle.

From where Polly and I were sitting on stools backstage, we could see the first few rows of the audience. I noticed Carole Lombard, Jack Benny, Patsy Kelly, Ann Harding, Van Heflin, Grady Sutton, Ginger Rogers, Leon Ames, Lyle Talbot, Roger Pilgrim, Arthur Sheekman, and Gloria Stuart out there. With the exception of Polly's father, who kept looking at his pocket watch and, probably, wondering when his daughter was ever going to get on stage, every one seemed to be enthralled by Groucho.

Jack Rolphs was sitting on the aisle in the third row of folding chairs and he was laughing and applauding in the right places. Behaving like a man who wasn't going to cancel our radio show and put me out of work.

". . . are there?" Polly had apparently asked me a question.

"Hum?"

"How many operettas did Gilbert and Sullivan write anyway?"

"Far too many."

Looking on the bright side, we did have four weeks to fiddle with the show. Trouble was, I thought the scripts were fine just the way I was doing them now. So did Groucho, who went over the first drafts with me every week and made suggestions and a few rude remarks.

Polly, who was dressed up in one of her frilly party dresses, stood up. "Does he really intend to wear that funny hat when we sing our duet at the end of my act?"

"It isn't exactly a funny hat," I said in my best avuncular manner. "When Nelson Eddy donned that hat in *Rose Marie,* he was deadly serious."

"Have you ever known Groucho to be serious about anything?"

"Well, outside of Gilbert and Sullivan and pastrami sandwiches, no."

"My father wants me to come across sweet and dignified tonight."

"Don't worry, you're both, Polly."

"The Zansky Brothers are supposed to be out there in the audience," she told me, sounding nervous. "They run Paragon Pictures, you know."

"I know," I answered. "So you're really going to sign with Paragon?"

"We're on the brink of signing," Polly said, smiling. "According to my father, everybody at Paragon likes my voice as much as Colonel Mullens does."

"Then you're going to get a nice deal out of the Zanskys I imagine."

She leaned closer to me. "I'll be pulling down almost as much as Deanna Durbin," she confided.

"That's terrific."

"I may not be quite as pretty as Deanna, but when it comes to my singing—well, I'm just about her equal."

A real uncle would have caught the hint and assured the pudgy girl that she was every bit as cute as Deanna Durbin. I considered it, but decided that while I wasn't above lying to sponsors and actors, I wasn't ready to start lying to kids.

Instead I said, "Your mother must be pleased, too."

"She is, very much." Polly lowered her voice. "I'm going to work out some way to share with her all this money I'm going to be making. My father says he's all for that."

"How's Frances feeling? Can we talk to her, do you think, tomorrow sometime?"

Polly gave a negative shake of her head. "She's better, but Dr. Steinberg says she really has to take it easy for at least a couple more days."

Out on the stage Groucho had stopped singing and strumming his guitar. The audience applauded enthusiastically, some of them even shouted approval.

"Oh, please, dear God," murmured Polly, "no more encores."

After holding up a hand for silence, Groucho stepped closer to the microphone. "I'm deeply touched by your ovation," he told the crowd. "And two or three of you also touched me for five bucks on the way in. Now we come to the high-class portion of the evening, which will bring you a very gifted young lady whom I have the pleasure of working with each week on that highly rated comedy show, *Groucho Marx, Private Eye*. A show, let me add, brilliantly written by the incomparable Frank Denby without any help from home or from any relatives of the sponsor or over educated New York snake oil salesmen." He directed his false smile directly at Jack Rolphs. "Without further ado, folks, here's the Songbird of Southern California—Miss Polly Pilgrim."

She squeezed my hand. "Please, tell him not to wear the hat," she said and walked out onto the stage.

He wore the hat.

But it didn't spoil anything. Alone on the stage, Polly had won the audience over with a short program that mixed some classical stuff with popular ballads. She finished up with "Isn't It Romantic?," the Rogers & Hart tune that Jeanette MacDonald had introduced in *Love Me Tonight* a few years earlier. That got her a standing ovation.

When Groucho went bounding back onto the boards wearing the Mountie hat, it produced a nice laugh. So did his explanation of how he came by the hat and that he'd been promised that Nelson Eddy's blond wig was supposed to come with it.

He and Polly did about fifteen minutes. Her father, in his bland way, seemed pleased with her performance. I was pretty sure I'd spotted one of the Zansky Brothers out in the fourth row and he was obviously enjoying the whole thing.

For an encore Polly and Groucho did a duet version of "Isn't It Romantic?"

They took several bows, with Groucho upstaging her on most

of them. But then he placed her at the edge of the stage and withdrew and Polly got a hand of her own.

Standing beside me and watching Polly smile at the audience, Groucho observed, "She's better than Florence Nightingale."

"Florence Nightingale wasn't a singer."

"Didn't I say she was *better* than Florence Nightingale?" he said as Polly took another bow. "It's tough not being beautiful in this town. Or so I've heard."

"I know you're doing the master of ceremonies chores on this thing," I said, "but soon as it's over, Groucho, I'd really like to talk about our radio show. I'm worried that—"

"Don't fret or mope, Fauntleroy," he advised. "Well, I suppose you can mope a little, but only in the privacy of your room."

"Those admen unsettled me."

"Mere shleppers who'll return to the stone canyons of Manhattan in a few days and forget all about us."

"I don't think so. It's been my experience that advertising agencies never forget. So it—"

"Ah, what is this vision of beauty I see before me?" Groucho had turned and was looking back toward the partition.

Turning, I saw that Rita Hayworth, a pretty dark-haired young woman, had stepped through the door and was approaching us.

Groucho went bounding over and took her hand. "Margarita, my dear," he said, kissing the hand with considerable enthusiasm. "It's a thrill to encounter you again and a distinct honor to be in the same show with you."

"Thank you, Mr. Marx," she said in a shy voice.

"Is your dear father lurking about anywhere?"

"He's out in the audience," she answered. "The dressing rooms are so small, he couldn't join me in mine."

"What a pity. Well, fear not, my child, I'll look after you like

185

a doting parent," he promised. "Ah, and here comes Pollyanna now. As soon as we sweep the vegetables off the stage, I'll introduce you to your adoring audience."

"That would be nice, Mr. Marx." She withdrew her hand from his grip.

Polly ran up to Groucho and hugged him. "We were a hit, Groucho," she said, laughing.

"*You* were a hit, kiddo. I'm merely a bedraggled mountebank, whatever that is."

Polly hugged me, then headed for her dressing room.

Groucho spoke close to my ear. "After I introduce this Cansino lass," he said in a whisper, "I'm going to watch her act. Then I'll join her and do my famous tango number with her."

"She may not want you intruding on the act."

"Nonsense, there hasn't been a tango dancer like me since Valentino," he said. "Hang around or come back after the encores and we can chat about your senseless worries concerning our show, Rollo."

"I'll wander around the park for a while."

He nodded, patted Rita Hayworth on her left buttock and went trotting out on the stage to introduce her.

She shook her head, sighing. "There's nobody else like him."

"Not on this continent, though they claim to have found one in the wilds of Australia." I wished her luck and eased my way out through a back flap in the tent.

There was a shutdown peanut wagon sitting on the grass just outside the tent. Two large guys in dark overcoats and gray hats were standing near it. The nearest concessions were closed and there were no other people in this stretch of the amusement park.

The larger of the two men grinned at me. "You're Frank Denby," he said.

Since it wasn't a question, I didn't feel obliged to answer. "And you?"

"Someone wants to talk with you, Frank," he informed me.

"Can he wait?" I pointed a thumb at the tent. "I'm supposed to stay close to the entertainment."

The other man had his right hand in his overcoat pocket. "He wants to see you right now," he explained. "We'll take you to him."

They took me to him.

Twenty-five

He was handsome but short.

"I'm Jack Cortez," he said and held out his hand.

Since there were two large guys in dark overcoats and gray hats standing near him with their right hands in their coat pockets and since I had a similar escort, being cordial seemed to be the thing to do.

"Pleased to me you." I shook the gangster's hand.

"I understand you know Vince Salermo."

"A little. Visited his gambling ship last year."

We were gathered in front of the cyclone fence that guarded the entrance to the Devil's Express Roller Coaster. A crudely lettered sign had been taped to the gate, explaining OUT OF OR-DER.

On the other side of the gate, however, a forlorn-looking fat man in coveralls was standing uneasily on the control platform with a large man in a dark overcoat and gray hat close beside him. The string of bright-lit red and gold cars sat on the tracks next to the boarding platform and looked ready to go roaring over the rising and falling course.

Scatterings of the Colonel's party guests passed a few yards off, but nobody came close enough for me to try to indicate that I was in trouble.

Cortez smiled. "I've been wanting to have a nice long talk with you, Frank," he informed me.

"Tonight, Jack, is not the best time," I said. "Colonel Mullens expects me to stay close to the tent until—"

"We'll go for a little ride."

"A ride?" There I was asking terse questions again.

He pointed at the roller coaster with his thumb. "I've loved these damn things ever since I was a kid and went to Coney Island," he explained. "The gentlemen who run Playland are friends of mine and I arranged to have a special ride tonight. A private trip that I'd like you to join me on, Frank."

"That's very thoughtful, Jack." I glanced up at the trestles that went rising up beyond the platform. "The thing is, I'm not all that fond of roller coasters. For a conversation I'm really at my best on nice solid ground."

He smiled. "We'll ride the roller coaster."

My two men in overcoats guided me to the gate and one of Cortez's overcoated men opened it wide.

Cortez climbed up to the steps that led to the boarding area. "The third car's my favorite," he said over his shoulder. "Is that all right with you, Frank?"

"Could we maybe just sit on the platform here and have our talk?"

My escorts took hold of an arm each and, quite swiftly, got me installed in the front row of seats in the third car.

Cortez settled into the seat beside me. "You've got to strap on your safety belt," he instructed, attaching his. "Otherwise you might go falling out."

I buckled myself in.

His two bodyguards climbed into the seats behind us. My two remained on the ground.

"Ever ride the Devil's Express before, Frank?"

"No, Jack. As I mentioned, I don't much like roller coasters." I tapped a spot just above my right ear. "It's a balance thing and—"

"Funny, I thought everybody liked roller coasters." Leaning back, Cortez gazed up into the night sky. "That wind really cleared things up. Look at all those stars."

I looked. Already I was, even though the roller coaster cars were sitting still, commencing to feel uneasy in my stomach. "What exactly did you want to talk about?"

"Excuse me a moment." He waved to the henchman who was overseeing the roller-coaster operator and pointed upward.

The nervous man in coveralls threw a switch, the cars quivered, lurched, and started to climb up the tracks toward the first peak on the route.

Unobtrusively, I caught hold of the edge of the seat on the side away from Cortez. I was already feeling dizzy.

He laughed. "This is just great," he observed. "Are you a Catholic, Frank?"

"No, but I'd like a Christian burial."

We were picking up speed, climbing closer to the initial peak. "Relax, Frank, nobody's going to do you any harm at this time," he assured me. "I'm a Catholic myself. It may sound strange, considering what you've probably heard about me and my reputation, but I was an altar boy in Brooklyn when I was a kid. Celebrated the mass almost every week for three, four years." He leaned back to study the night sky again.

"I'm not quite getting the drift of this." I swallowed a few times, trying to get rid of the sour taste that was starting to build up.

"Catholics believe that God gives all of us a vocation soon as we're born."

We hit the top with a jolt, hesitated a few seconds, and then went plunging downward.

I had to grit my teeth and concentrate on my inner workings to keep from giving in to a growing impulse to vomit.

Cortez took out a cigarette and lit it with a gold lighter. "For example, what God gifted me with was a vocation to be a businessman. Making a lot of money, that was my calling. I realized that early and it helped me to follow the right path in life."

"Um," I managed to reply without risking opening my mouth.

Cold wind seemed to be pushing at me, trying to yank me clear out of the plummeting car.

He tapped me on the upper arm, causing me to flinch. "You were given a different vocation, Frank."

We were nearly at the bottom of our first plunge and I became convinced we wouldn't survive. That instead, all of the bright-painted cars would go flying off into the darkness beyond the lights. Carefully, I closed my eyes and hoped Cortez wouldn't notice it.

"Your vocation is to be a writer, that's what God wants you to do. Your calling is to type stories for newspapers and turn out scripts for radio shows."

My stomach seemed unhappy with its present location and was trying to break clean out of my body. When I opened my eyes again we were rushing up toward the next pinnacle.

"Take Groucho Marx. God wants him to be a funnyman. His

192

mission in life is to make people laugh, at least those people who think he's funny."

My digestive system was becoming unhappy about the root beer I'd drunk right before the entertainment started. I opened my mouth, hoping that if I sucked in some gasps of cold air it would calm my stomach.

"It's everyone's duty to stick with the assigned vocation. That's what God expects of us."

We were at the second peak. The rattling, shrieking drop was even worse than the previous one. I shut my mouth and my eyes.

"What I'm explaining here, Frank, is very simple. We all of us have to stick with what we're destined to do. You are a writer, Groucho is a comedian."

Root beer laced with bile came surging up my throat. I closed my mouth again with a biting snap. The stuff collected in my mouth, some of it spilling out over my lower lip.

"Neither one of you is a *detective,*" said Cortez patiently. "If you keep trying to be detectives, Frank, it's going against God's will. Worse, it goes against my wishes. What you have to do, you *and* Groucho, is to stop messing around with the Benninger kill."

I intended to reply with, "So you did have something to do with that, huh?"

Instead, which was probably just as well, as soon as I opened my mouth, I vomited. I managed to get my head over the edge of the speeding car just in time.

"Hey, watch that shit," complained one of the bodyguards behind us.

The other bodyguard just laughed.

My impressions of the rest of the ride, which felt as though it lasted several hours and rushed me up several miles into the cold night and down even deeper below the surface of the Earth, are somewhat hazy. I'm nearly certain I threw up at least once more. Cortez kept lecturing me.

A headache hit me and my bones ceased to feel comfortable inside my flesh.

The ride ended at last, though the roar of it was still strong in my head.

Sometime later I found myself alone, abandoned on the grass by the peanut wagon.

I was eventually able to arrange myself in a standing position. After concentrating, I remembered how to walk and, staggering and swaying some, I went through the rear flap into the tent.

When I reached the back stage area, Polly saw me and came hurrying over to me. "You look awful, Frank," she said, putting an arm around me.

"That's the appropriate look," I told her in a dry, croaky voice. "Could you find Groucho for me?"

She got me arranged on a stool. "You're going to have to wait a bit," she said. "He's back on the stage doing more junk from Gilbert and Sullivan."

Twenty-six

Groucho pulled his Cadillac up in front of Jane's beach cottage. The big car shimmied when he hit the brakes, a fender scraped against the curb. "This would certainly be a splendid time for me to exclaim, 'Aha, I see it all now!' " he said, turning off the engine. "I do see quite a bit and I think we've got a fair idea of what really happened to Dr. Benninger and why."

"Yeah, but we don't have much in the way of proof." I reached for the handle of my door. "We can't go to the Bayside cops with what we suspect, because Sergeant Branner is in charge of that end of things and even the few honest cops I know aren't exactly willing to cross him."

"Stir not, young sir," he cautioned. "I'll fit around and help extract you from the vehicle."

"I'm okay," I told him without much conviction. The headache was hanging on and I still felt somewhere between mildly woozy and mildly dizzy.

Groucho, in his civilian guise now, hopped from the driver's seat and came trotting around the nose of his car.

I, meantime, had opened the door and swung partway out.

It was a few minutes short of eleven. The wind was still

blowing in hard across the dark Pacific.

"One of the Colonel's loyal underlings, by the way, will drive your car over here later in the evening and leave it in the driveway," Groucho said. "I believe it's the same clever lad who invented the sixth flavorful flavor."

Taking my arm, he helped me onto the sidewalk and up the path to the porch. "Would you like me to tell the lady of the house that you look this way because you got plastered drinking highballs with a gang of tattooed sailors down in San Pedro?" he inquired. "That sounds a mite more rugged than admitting you got giddy riding on a roller coaster."

"We'll stick to the truth," I said. "I seem to be getting fewer and fewer opportunities to do that."

"I'll keep mum about the fact that you fraternized with a Mullens Maiden."

"At least I didn't climb up a ladder with one."

"Obviously you have no concept of what's involved in being a Boy Scout. If I don't perform at least one good deed each day, they take my knapsack away, break my—"

"Frank, are you okay?" Jane had heard our approach and yanked the door open.

"He got drunk with a gang of tattooed sailors down in San Pedro," explained Groucho.

"No, he didn't." She put an arm around me. "What really happened?"

"I had one of those nausea attacks, this time from riding a roller coaster." I let her help me across the cottage threshold. "It ought to be gone in a few more hours."

She guided me to the sofa and arranged me there. "Since you know you have a problem, that was kind of stupid, wasn't it?"

"He was coerced," Groucho told her.

"Who did that?"

I answered, "Jack Cortez and some of his goons."

She inhaled sharply, took a step back. "Jesus, Frank, did they try to throw you off the top of that damn thing?"

"Not this trip, although they didn't rule it out for some future jaunt."

"These thugs," put in Groucho, perching on the arm of the sofa, "are obviously annoyed by our activities."

"Hell, *I'm* annoyed by your activities," she said, scowling at each of us in turn. "I want you to help Frances London out of this mess, but not if you get killed in the process."

"I didn't get killed. I got an upset stomach and a headache," I reminded. "And I don't think Cortez planned that, since he doesn't know about my balance problem."

"Reluctantly, children, I must tear myself away from this cozy domestic scene," announced Groucho. "I have a rendezvous with fate. That is, if you accept the theorem that you can meet fate in a bawdy house and—"

"You're still going to try to contact Maggie Barnes?"

"We need something tangible to go to the law with, Rollo," he said. "Maggie isn't the most praiseworthy of young ladies, but lord knows she's tangible."

"But the gunman who shot at us might be working for the same gang that runs that bordello, Groucho. You better be—"

"Whoa, wait, stop." Jane held up her hand in a traffic cop gesture. "Who shot at you? Was this on the roller-coaster ride?"

"Could you fix me a Bromo-Seltzer?" I requested.

"Not until you thoroughly explain the shooting business, Frank."

Groucho left the chair arm. "A person or persons unknown,

Miss Janey, took a few shots at us," he said. "That occurred in that temple of art known as the Filmland Wax Museum while we were admiring a handsome and awe-inspiring tableau of wax replicas of your humble servant and my not-so-humble siblings. Frank's fast action in shoving a feeble old man, namely, me, to the floorboards, saved my life and—"

"Shot a few times?" Jane was picking up my habit of asking terse questions.

"We didn't get hurt," I said. "This guy, whoever he was— we didn't get a look at him—was probably only trying to scare us."

"Yet you just now, Frank, warned Groucho that he might get shot."

"Shot *at*," I corrected. "I'm firmly convinced, Jane, that a Bromo-Seltzer would help."

"What you actually need to settle your stomach is a cup of peppermint tea." She rose.

"I wasn't aware," observed Groucho, "that tea came in flavorful flavors."

"It's something my aunt sends me."

"The dishtowel aunt," I added.

"As much as I'd love to stick around and watch you brew tea, Miss Danner, I must be going." Bowing in her direction, he shuffled over to the door. "I'll telephone you bright and early in the morning, Rollo—around noon—and we'll confer."

"If you survive tonight."

"I'd hate to tell you how many nights in houses of ill repute that I've survived, young feller." He opened the door. "The correct answer is three, which will be printed upside down in tomorrow's bulldog edition of *The Bayside Shopping News*. Should you not have a bulldog, you're pretty much out of luck."

198

He stepped outside into a cold gust of wind. The door flapped shut.

Jane stood watching me for a few seconds. "You sure don't look very good."

"So I keep hearing."

"You won't pass out while I make us each a cup of tea?"

"If I do," I promised, "I'll try not to fall on anything breakable."

Twenty-seven

Groucho said, "Good evening, I'm Otto Heffel."

The man who'd opened the white door of the bordello was built along the lines of a frequenter of muscle beach and was wearing pinstripe gray slacks, a black dress shirt, and wide yellow suspenders. He surveyed Groucho briefly through the foot-wide opening. "Take a hike, Otto," he suggested. "This is a private club and I don't know you."

Handing him the letter he'd gotten from Nathanael West earlier in the day, Groucho said, "I realized that, so I had one of your regular customers write me this letter of introduction."

The big, wide man took the envelope, slid out the letter, and unfolded it. "You know Pep West?"

"We're lodge brothers."

"Nice guy, but a little screwy. He comes around quite a lot, you know, but never once goes upstairs," said the bouncer. "What Pep likes to do is sit around the parlor and just talk to the girls. Says he's writing a book."

"I do believe he is."

"A book about what?"

"A book about Hollywood," answered Groucho. "May I cross the threshold?"

"Hold you damn horses, Otto." He studied the letter. " 'This will introduce my old friend, Otto Heffel of Ventura. He's a true gentleman and a big spender. Yours truly, Nathanael West.' " The bouncer refolded the letter, put it back into the envelope and returned that to Groucho. "Okay, Otto, I guess you're kosher."

"Rabbis use me as a touchstone." He entered the carpeted hallway. The scents of face powder and perfume were strong in the air.

Taking hold of Groucho just above the elbow, the big man escorted him into the parlor. "Wait in there," he instructed and left.

The room was dimly illuminated and the shades and the bulbs on the two floor lamps were pale pink. The three flowered sofas and two fat armchairs were unoccupied. A tall, ample woman in a navy blue evening dress was squatting to turn up the volume on the large Atwater Kent radio next to the small empty fireplace. It was a Count Basie band remote broadcast.

Groucho coughed into his hand. "Do I have the pleasure of addressing Mrs. Ferguson herself?"

The woman rose and turned to scrutinize him. "No, she's flat on her ass with whooping cough," she told him. "I'm the manager. Constance is my name."

Groucho showed her his letter.

After reading it, she asked, "You like to talk to girls, too?"

"As a preliminary only."

The manager wore a dead white powder and her face and shoulders looked as though they'd been dipped in flour. Her lipstick was a purplish red. "You look like somebody," she said, coming closer to him.

"It's from taking a Dale Carnegie course. Before that I looked like nobody."

"No, I mean you look like that guy in the movies except he's got a moustache."

"Oh, you mean Clark Gable." Groucho nodded. "I was getting mistaken for him so often that I had to shave off my own moustache, Constance."

"Nope, I mean you look something like that funny guy."

"You're thinking of William Powell. Lots of people have commented on the resemblance."

"Hell, never mind. I'll think of it eventually," she said. "What sort of girl would you like, Oscar?"

"Otto," he corrected.

"Otto it is. Now, let me tell you right off the reel that we don't employ any kids here," she said, hands on hips. "There's not one of our girls who's not over eighteen. We also don't have any Chinks. Far as I'm concerned, we could provide Chinks and Japs for our clients. Mrs. Ferguson, though—"

"Well, actually, Pep West recommended a young lady to me," Groucho broke in. "Her name was . . . um . . . what the devil was it? Oh, yes, Maggie Barnes."

"You're in luck, Otto. This is one of the nights Maggie's on duty." She returned to the radio. "A very pretty girl, awfully affectionate. She looks sort of like that movie actress that just killed the doctor." Constance opened the thin ledger book that sat atop the radio.

With the Basie band Jimmy Rushing was singing "I'm Gonna Move to the Outskirts of Town."

"I do hope she's available," said Groucho in what he hoped was a timid voice.

"Bingo, she is." She looked back at him over her white shoulder. "That'll be fifty bucks."

"Fifty dollars? I don't want to hire her by the week."

"Fifty bucks. This isn't some hand-job joint in Tijuana, after all." Constance put her hands on her hips again and frowned at him. "That's fifty for us, plus the ten-dollar towel fee and then whatever tip you want to leave for Maggie."

Groucho took some folded bills from the pocket of his checkered sport coat. He counted off sixty dollars and, reluctantly, passed them to the manager.

As her hand closed over the bills, a thin Negro maid entered the room and said to Groucho, "If you'll follow me, sir."

"It's been a pleasure chatting with you, Constance. I hope I'll see you on my way out."

"You might. Enjoy yourself, Otto."

He followed the maid into the hall and up one flight of stairs. After nodding at a door with the numerals 232 painted on it, she handed him a rolled-up white towel and two contraceptives. "It's all right to tip, sir."

Groucho gave her a dollar bill. When she was on her way downstairs, he knocked on Maggie Barnes's door.

"Come in, sweetheart," invited a familiar voice.

He went in.

Maggie Barnes said, "I'd be risking my life. They'd kill me." She was sitting on the edge of the bed, wearing a black slip.

"Who'd kill you?" Groucho sat in the room's only chair.

"The people who sure as hell don't want me to talk."

"I'm offering you some money right now." He leaned forward, hands clasped between his legs. "Frances London's daughter, Polly Pilgrim, is a very successful performer," he said. "Polly's father comes from a wealthy family. If you make a statement, Maggie, they'll see to it that you get a handsome reward."

"What're they going to do, toss the dough into my grave along with the pallbearers' gloves?"

The bedroom window was open at the bottom and the wind was fluttering the peach-colored lace curtains.

"What you know might be enough to put them in jail. That way—"

She laughed. "Did you ever hear of the Mob, Groucho? They call them that because there's a whole lot of them," she told him. "You put a couple in the can, there's dozens more still on the outside. They're like cockroaches."

"The police can protect a witness."

Her left eye nearly closed and she tilted her head. "This wouldn't be the Bayside cops you're talking about? Yeah, they'd protect me just swell."

"Was it Branner who had you pretend to be Frances London and bang on Dr. Benninger's door that night?"

"Who says I did anything like that? The witnesses all said it was Frances herself."

"Branner makes a habit of covering up for hoodlums," said Groucho. "Now, Maggie, I'm a witness to your passing me a death threat. Did Branner hire you for that job, too? Or did you deal directly with Jack Cortez?"

"You really, Groucho, ought to stick to the movies," she advised him, crossing her bare legs. "You're in way over your head."

"So are you, Maggie my dear," he pointed out. "Think about this, if you will. I intend to keep digging into this until I can prove Frances is innocent. That means eventually I should be able to prove you were involved, too. At that point, it's pretty likely they'll arrest you as an accessory."

"Jail's still better than a cemetery."

Groucho said, "Okay, let's talk about your profession."

"I'm a hooker. So?"

"I thought you were an actress."

She laughed again. "Jesus, Groucho, do you know how many guys have promised to get me in pictures?"

"You're not good enough for movies yet," he told her. "But I can help you get hired for some kind of show business job. A job that's at least a few notches above turning tricks and stooging for hoodlums and crooked cops."

She uncrossed her legs, sitting up straighter on the chenille bedspread. "This is just a line of crap," she said. "Your goddamned brother Zeppo practically tossed me out on my butt. It's been the same with a lot of other agents."

"You help me, I'll help you."

After a few seconds, she said, "No, it's too dangerous."

He left the chair, easing closer to the blonde. "That was you pretending to be a drunken Frances, wasn't it?"

She looked toward the door, then the window. "I'll deny saying this later," she said. "But, yes."

"Where was Dr. Benninger?"

She shrugged. "I don't know. Nobody ever came to the door."

"Dead already inside the house maybe?"

"He might've been," she conceded. "But I didn't know anything about that. What they told me was that somebody wanted to ruin Frances's reputation, not frame her for murder. But, you know, once you do it—doesn't matter what you thought or what you were told."

"Who hired you, Maggie?"

She turned her head so that she wouldn't meet his eyes. "He'll kill me."

"Just tell me. Then maybe I can find some other way to prove it."

"It was Sergeant Branner," she said quietly.

"Did he pay you to do it?"

"A little bit," she answered. "Mainly I did it because I didn't want him to beat me up again."

"Was he taking orders from Jack Cortez?"

"That part I don't know," the blonde answered. "He's done a lot of stuff for Cortez in the past so it's sure possible."

"Okay, now what about—"

"Shit," she said.

The pink-shaded bedside lamp had started blinking.

"That a signal?" he asked.

"Means a raid. We have them now and then." She ran to the closet, grabbed out a black chiffon dress and pulled it on over her head. "If Branner's along on this one and he finds you and me together—"

"What's out that window?"

"The roof of the garages," Maggie answered. "We can, if you're up to it, slide down that and into the yard of the joint behind us. I've done it."

"Tonight, my dear, I feel divinely inspired." Loping over, he jerked the window open wide. Night wind smacked him in the face.

"Where's my shoes? Where's my goddamned shoes?"

Downstairs a loud pounding had commenced on the front door.

"We'll have to do a barefoot escape." Groucho took her arm,

tugged her to the window. "You want to go first, my pet?"

"Sure, since I know the route." She swung one leg over the windowsill. "It's kind of steep, Groucho, so don't trip and go sliding." Maggie stepped out onto the slanting shingle roof.

Groucho thrust his head through the opening. He could hear cars pulling up in front of the bordello.

Maggie was on all fours, working her way down the roof backward.

"No time to have my stuntman do this one." He went lurching out of the bedroom.

Inside the room the door came slamming open and a voice warned, "Stop or I'll shoot."

Twenty-eight

I sat up suddenly in bed, heart beating fast.

Beside me Jane went on sleeping, in that huddled position she always got into eventually.

Looking toward the darkened bedroom windows, I listened.

Now I heard footsteps moving quietly down the driveway.

Probably what had awakened me was nothing more than the noises that went with one of Colonel Mullens' people returning my car.

I eased carefully out of bed anyway and light-footed it over to where I'd left my clothes. I put on my trousers, shirt, and shoes.

Jane didn't wake up.

When I got to the front windows I got a glimpse of somebody shutting the door on the passenger side of a dark sedan after climbing inside. Lights off, the car went rolling off along the night street.

Very carefully I opened the front door and stepped out on the porch. From the right-hand side you could see the drive.

My yellow Plymouth was parked next to the cottage, the

imitation raccoon tail hanging from the antenna looking especially bedraggled.

Sitting on the running board was a large shopping bag.

"What the hell is that?"

I went down the steps, stood watching my car and the mysterious package.

The fat calico cat from three houses over emerged from the deep shadow under my returned car. Standing up on her chubby hind legs, she started poking at the bag with a paw.

If there were some sort of explosive device in that sack, I ought to shoo the cat off. I would, though, have felt silly yelling, "Get away from there, Peachy Pet!" at 1:00 A.M.

Crossing the dew-stained lawn with shoes and no socks gave me damp ankles.

I was still about ten feet from my coupé, when Peachy Pet gave the bag an extra exuberant smack. It teetered and fell to the driveway.

Several boxes of Mullens Pudding tumbled out.

The surprised cat dived back under my car.

"You've got a serious case of the heebie-jeebies," I told myself.

A note came with the two dozen boxes—in all five flavorful flavors—of pudding. It read, "Hope you're recovering from your ordeal and it's not simply because you're going to do me an awfully big favor, but because I think you're a very nice person and I'm very glad that chance, unless you believe in predestination, which I'm not really sure I do—"

"Victoria," I said and didn't bother to finish the letter.

Gathering up the scattered boxes, I tossed them back in the sack along with the note. I carried the stuff over and left it on the lowest porch step.

Hands in pockets I walked the short distance down to the beach.

The wind was still strong, the black water choppy. The foamy surf that came washing in across the sand glowed faintly.

I found a smooth hunk of driftwood above the reach of the surf and sat down. There was a half-moon tonight and what seemed like an extra amount of stars.

"I'd hate to lose the damn show," I said aloud. "I can probably get another one going, but not with Groucho and not for this kind of money. You've got to face it, Groucho's the one who was able to get me this salary. On your own, you're not likely to—"

"Pardon me, sir, but we're looking for an escaped lunatic."

"What sort of lunatic?"

"This fellow likes to freeze his backside on chilly beaches while reciting rambling monologues."

"What's he look like?"

"According to the description we've got, he's not much to look at."

"And not much to see?"

"That's him."

"Haven't seen him. Sit down, Jane, there's room on this log."

"Unlike this loon I was telling you about, I don't have a morbid desire to freeze my fanny," She stepped closer to where I was sitting. "Come home with me now and I'll fix us some hot cocoa."

I left the log. "Sorry I woke you."

"You didn't. It must've been the people bringing your car home. Just takes me longer to wake up than it does you."

"After I went out to see if it was my car, I decided to wander down here for a while."

"Who's Victoria?"

"I was going to tell you about her. She's a Mullens Maiden."

"They keep a supply of virgins around to sacrifice on important occasions?"

Side by side, we started back toward the cottage. "The Mullens Maidens are sort of like the Goldwyn Girls or maybe the Wampus Babies," I explained. "Only they hand out free samples of pudding. When a new market opens or there's a party or convention."

"And why's this particular Mullens Maiden eternally grateful to you?"

I halted. "Hey, I thought by now you were aware that I was completely and eternally committed to you," I told her. "This girl is about twenty, wants to be an actress. She's got an interesting sort of voice and style of speech. I'd like to audition her for the part of Groucho's new secretary on our show."

Jane moved a few steps away, stood eyeing me. "Okay, I trust you," she decided after a moment. "It's merely that when a pretty girl comes by in the middle of the night and leaves pudding on the doorstep, I get curious."

"Actually, she left it on the running board of my car. She must've driven one of the cars over here."

"Is Victoria aware of your undying devotion to me?"

"I told her that my heart was spoken for, showed her the brand on my flank."

"Good." Jane returned to my side and took my hand. "What were you talking to yourself about down by the seashore?"

"I'm worried about our radio show, Jane." Because I'd been recuperating from my roller-coaster ride, I hadn't gotten around to telling her about my encounter with the Colonel, his talented youngest son, and the East Coast admen.

"I don't think you have to worry."

By this time we were sitting across from each other in the breakfast nook with our mugs of cocoa.

"The show's never been as popular as Benny or Edgar Bergen or Burns and Allen or—"

"There's a good living to be made by people who aren't at the very top of the list."

"Sponsors don't think that way, Jane."

"Sure, but I still don't think you have to brood so much about this."

"Okay, I swear I'll brood through the night and into the morning, Jane, and then I'll quit forever," I promised, holding up my right hand. "I'll become a tourist attraction in Southern California, Ripley will come courting. When I stroll along Hollywood Boulevard, people will applaud and cry out, 'There goes Frank Denby—he hasn't brooded in over six months.' "

"Finish your cocoa," she advised, "and let's go to bed."

Twenty-nine

Groucho's departure down across the steep rooftop of the bordello garage didn't go quite as smoothly as he was hoping.

After scrambling out of the window and ignoring Sergeant Branner's command to stop, he dropped into a crouch and started working his way downward.

There were no outside lights nearby and the pink light from the bedroom didn't spill very far.

The sergeant had reached the window now. "Come on back in here, you," he shouted.

Paying no attention, Groucho kept moving. In fact, he moved with considerable rapidity. He slipped, lost his balance and his purchase and went whizzing downward across the roof toward the dark yard that belonged to the house immediately behind Mrs. Ferguson's establishment.

Maggie had reached the edge and lowered herself over it. She was dangling from the edge, bare feet feeling for the upper side of the garage window frame. "Jesus, Groucho," she whispered as she saw him come sailing toward her.

Summoning up what acrobatic skills he'd attained during his vaudeville days, he twisted sideways as he plunged over the rim of the roof. He managed to grab the drainpipe.

As he got both hands locked round it and gripping tightly, the pipe groaned and creaked. Then it began to tear free of its moorings and break from the garage side.

Groucho, as though clinging to a giant metal arm, was lowered, in rattling jerks, to the dark lawn below.

He let go of the drain pipe, tripped over a tricycle he hadn't previously been aware of. He landed hard on his back side.

The bell on the tricycle tingled as he bumped his elbow against it.

From up above came three shots. "Around back, get some men around back!" It sounded as though the sergeant was still up in the abandoned bedroom.

"Did you break your damn leg or anything?" Maggie had come quickly over the damp grass to him.

"That's a very good question, young lady, and I do hope it won't stump our experts." Taking hold of the hand she offered, he pulled himself to his feet. "At a rough guess, I'd say I'm as close to physical perfection as I ever was."

"Then let's get our asses the hell away from here." Gripping his arm, she started running him toward the gate in the picket fence. "That sounds like Sergeant Branner up there hollering. He catches us together, you can be damn sure he'll think of a good legal reason to shoot us both."

"I had the foresight," said Groucho when they reached the night sidewalk, "to park my car a couple blocks to the north of here. If we scurry in that direction, we ought to be able to drive to safer climes before the posse catches up with us."

*   *   *

216

By the time Groucho's Cadillac reached the outskirts of Hermosa Beach, a short way down the coast from Bayside, a light fog was hanging over the highway.

"The odds are the son of a bitch recognized you," Maggie was saying. She was huddled in the passenger seat, knees up and a plaid lap robe wrapped around her legs and bare feet. "So he can find me through you."

Groucho, dead cigar clutched in his teeth, was hunched at the wheel and squinting out into the misty night. "Keep your eyes open for the Big Orange," he told her. "And cease fretting about dear Sergeant Branner."

"He *saw* you at the cat house."

"No, he saw my backside going out a window," he corrected. "And Branner doesn't know me anywhere well enough to recognize its unique qualities."

"Somebody tipped him you were there, though."

"Probably the estimable Constance," he said. "But all she can have informed Branner is that a chap resembling Groucho Marx had dropped by to pay his respects. Granted, I do resemble Groucho Marx, but I'm not the only—"

"She can identify you—in a lineup or from the witness stand."

"It won't ever come to that."

"What makes you think he won't—"

"As long as he doesn't have any idea where you are, Maggie dear, he isn't going to risk annoying me too much," he explained. "Because Branner can't be sure you haven't told me all about his involvement in the murder of Dr. Benninger."

"What I know doesn't tie him to that directly."

"It certainly links him with an attempt to frame Frances London," he said. "Aha!"

217

Up ahead on the foggy night highway loomed the roadside juice stand he was seeking. The stand had been built in the shape of a giant orange. Floating above the tin structure was a sign announcing BIG ORANGE—FRESH JUICE 10 CENTS! Although the service window was shut, a slice of light showed along its lower edge.

Groucho swung onto the gravel area in front of the huge orange.

"I never drink orange juice unless it's spiked with gin," commented Maggie, rearranging her blanket.

"After we stop here, my dear, we'll drop by the Big Gin Bottle." He eased out of the car. "Stay here."

"Don't worry, I'm not planning to take a quick dip in the goddamned ocean."

When Groucho tapped on the tin window cover, it swung up and open with a rattling rasp. "You better be the guy Leroy telephoned about and got me up out of bed for," said the sleepy-looking young man who was frowning out at him.

"I am he." He held out his hand. "The keys?"

"Leroy said you'd give me twenty bucks for my trouble."

"No, as I understand it he promised you ten."

"Shit, it's after midnight."

Groucho produced a twenty-dollar bill. "Leroy better not have promised you anything else, my lad."

From a pocket of his jeans, the thin youth took a ring with two brass keys dangling from it. "Biggest one is the front door, other one's the garage. Got that?"

"I dearly hope so or otherwise I'm liable to park my car in the living room."

"Huh?"

Groucho made a give-me-those motion and the young man

218

tossed him the keys. "And where exactly is this luxurious villa?"

"Jesus, didn't they even tell you that?"

"I was told you'd tell me."

"It's easy. You go down the highway to the next road and turn left. Go uphill about two miles and then take another left on Ellison Road. It's the second house on the right, number 914. Mission style. Good night." He shut the window with a tinny bang.

Groucho, jingling the house keys, trotted back to his car. "We're near our goal," he said as he started the engine.

"This is the most elaborate shack up I've ever been tangled up with."

"This is not shacking up, dear child. This is hiding out." The Cadillac wobbled onto the misty night highway. "Something you're doing alone."

"It's late, Groucho," she said, touching his shoulder. "Since you've driven all the way down here, you might as well spend the night."

"If only I hadn't taken a vow of chastity this very morning," he said. "Attend to me, Maggie dear, and make sure you forget romance and concentrate on keeping above ground." He turned the big car onto the indicated side road. "Tomorrow morning a gentleman named Ethan Gumpertz will call on you at this hideaway to take your statement. He's an attorney and a notary public."

"Aren't you coming back with him?"

"Probably not, but I'll certainly visit you during your stay."

"I'm going to go stir crazy if I have to live here very long."

"Much better than occupying a hole in the ground up in one of the canyons."

They climbed away from the beach.

"Your brother Zeppo knows the guy who owns this dump?"

"A client of his who's in New York starring in a hit play," answered Groucho. "I thought of this place while cudgeling my brain for someplace to hide you. The play's a hit, about incest in New England, and this chap isn't likely to be back for another six months."

"Christ, I can't spend six months away from—"

"You probably won't have to hide out for more than a few days, Maggie." He turned onto Ellison Road. "Once we put Sergeant Branner away, then you'll—"

"Lots of people have tried to knock him out of the box and he's still pretty much running things in Bayside."

"He hasn't come up against me before."

"Sure, he has. Last year."

"Okay, all right. Once before, yes, but this time we'll get him for sure." Groucho parked in the driveway beside the large tile-and-stucco house. "Justice is going to triumph."

"We'll see," she said. "And what am I going to do about clothes and a pair of shoes?"

Thirty

When I opened the opaque glass door and, dripping and soapy-eyed, stepped out onto the bath mat, I noticed Groucho perched on the closed toilet seat.

"If Jane still loves you after seeing you in your natural state, Rollo, then she is an extremely tolerant woman." He'd apparently been sitting there reading the Sunday funnies while waiting for me to finish my shower.

Wrapping a couple of large white terry-cloth towels around myself, I inquired, "What in the hell are you doing here?"

"Something unexpected has come up." He folded the comic section and rose from the seat.

"You weren't supposed to get in touch with me until around noon." I plucked my watch from the glass shelf beneath the medicine cabinet and strapped it to my damp wrist. "It's only ten-fifteen."

Groucho said, "Frances London has disappeared."

"Oh, Christ. Disappeared how?" I used one of my towels to dry my head.

"That's what we're going to journey to Manhattan Beach with all due haste to determine," he told me. "Pollyanna, sometimes known as the shiksa Fanny Brice, telephoned me half an hour ago. She'd been delivered to her mother's home by the family chauffeur in order to have breakfast with her. Frances wasn't in the house, there was no note of any kind, and Polly found signs of a struggle of some sort."

"Did she call the police?" Opening the door, I went into the bedroom.

"Not yet." Groucho followed me. "Keep in mind that Frances is out on bail and required to stay pretty much in the vicinity. At this point it's no use giving the cops cause for alarm. With firemen, you might want to give them cause for four alarms, but—"

"Somebody's grabbed her." I gathered up fresh clothes and retreated into the big closet to dress.

"That's my conclusion as well," he said. "Frances has no reason to skip bail."

"That we know of," I said. "But she's been under a lot of pressure, Groucho, and maybe that—"

"Spare me, Dr. Jung," he cut in. "The Frances I conferred with the other day in the calaboose is a rational woman. She sure isn't going to flee the country and leave her kid and her career behind."

"You're right, yeah," I conceded. "And I won't suggest that she went off on a binge either."

"Not voluntarily she didn't. But if the police come in at this point, they're going to conclude that Frances either jumped bail or went off on a toot," he said. "And this is such a serious matter that I'm not even going to suggest that she'd make better time if she went off in a taxi cab. Of course, Ginsburg the Human cannonball went off three times a day with an extra performance on Saturdays. Put a great strain on his wife."

I emerged, fully clothed, to find Groucho stretched out on his stomach atop the spread with the funnies covering my pillow. "I hope you haven't left footprints on the bedspread," I said.

"No, fear not, I wiped my boots on the curtains before assuming this fetching pose. When I worked for the Street and Smith publishing outfit in my youth, I had a job fetching prose, but that's another, and a far better, story. I later turned my experiences into a play I entitled *West Lynne* but the critics all agreed I'd gone off in the wrong direction." He folded up his comic section. "I was just catching up with the latest episode of *Hawkshaw the Detective*. He's a brilliant fellow who has an assistant who's even dimmer than you."

From the kitchen now came the aroma of fresh corn muffins. "I'm going to have breakfast before we go," I told him, leaving the bedroom.

"We can allow you exactly four minutes for that, Watso," he said, walking close behind me. "Unless you invite me to join you and then we can spare oodles of time."

Jane had a dishtowel tied around her slim waist, serving as an apron. It was one of those embroidered ones provided by the Fresno aunt and was covered with a great many too many appliqued kittens.

"The squire here," Groucho informed her, "has invited me to partake of your humble fare, Miss Jane."

"We're all out of humble fare. You'll take muffins and like them."

Groucho bowed toward her. "I'll run into the breakfast nook and make sure I get a good seat." He tucked the funnies up under his arm and went scooting away. "You two young things can then talk about me when I'm gone."

"He told me that Frances London seems to be missing," said

223

Jane after kissing me on the cheek. "What do you think it means?"

"Bigger and better trouble," I answered.

This isn't the best part of Manhattan Beach," I said as Groucho parked the Cadillac at the curb.

"There is no best part of Manhattan Beach," he said, exiting the car. "Something the civic fathers have long been sensitive about."

The small houses sat close together on forty-and sixty-foot lots and you couldn't see the ocean at all from this narrow twisting inland block.

The place Frances London lived in was a tired-looking wood-frame house. Cream-colored and trimmed in sea blue. The driveway was short and the tail end of the Pilgrim limousine parked in it hung out over the cracked sidewalk.

The Pilgrim chauffeur was sitting on the bottom step of the porch smoking a cigarette. "Hi, Frankie. Hello, Mr. Marx. Brat's inside."

"Anything new?" I asked as we climbed up to the front door.

He shrugged. "The lady's still missing."

Polly, tearful, wearing jeans and a pullover, opened the front door. "Groucho, I'm really glad you're here." She hugged him, then pulled him into the living room.

I went in and shut the door. "Your mother hasn't called?"

"No, Frank. I'm really awfully worried."

Groucho, hands behind his back, was slouching around the small, neat room. "No signs of violence here."

"Come along with me." Polly went over to an open doorway, beckoning us to follow.

Even though the curtains were drawn in the bedroom, you could see that there'd been some sort of fracas. A chair near the doorway lay on its side, the magazines that had been resting on it had gone sliding out across the rug. The bedside table had fallen, too, spilling two rental library books, an empty coffee mug, and a black metal alarm clock on the floor. The blankets and the top sheet had been pulled all the way down to the foot of the metal-frame bed.

"Look in the closet," said Polly, pointing.

Groucho eased along beside the bed and took a look. "Somebody yanked clothes off hangers in a less than careful manner," he observed. "Suitcases missing?"

"Two small ones," answered Polly. "But that's part of the frame-up, don't you see?"

"You think they gathered up a bunch of your mother's clothes and stuffed them into the suitcases to make it look like she was skipping town," he said. "But if she were really making a run for it, she wouldn't have left those two silk dresses crumpled up on the floor amidst those fallen hangers and she certainly wouldn't have taken only one slipper of that new pink pair."

"That's what I mean, Groucho." Polly sniffled, rubbed at her nose with her knuckles. "She was kidnapped, wasn't she?"

"She was pretty certainly forced to vacate the premises against her will."

"I'll show you the kitchen door now," offered Polly. "It was obviously jimmied."

Groucho was looking down at the fallen clock. Stopping he scooped it up and studied it, front and back. "Interesting, Rollo," he said after a moment.

"Oh, so?"

"Frances set the alarm to go off at seven-thirty this morning," he pointed out, tapping the clock. "It apparently did ring, but nobody turned it off and it ran down."

"Suggesting that she wasn't here when it started ringing?"

"Wasn't here or wasn't able to turn the thing off."

"So she was probably grabbed before seven-thirty."

"Unless she was still here and merely brushing her teeth or brewing a pot of coffee."

"She didn't do either." Polly nodded in the direction of the bathroom doorway. "Her toothbrush is in its glass and dry. Nothing was on the stove in the kitchen when I got here."

Nodding, Groucho set the clock back on the floor. "We'll have to ask the neighbors if they heard anything during the night or early morning hours," he said to me. "Do you know any of the nearby citizenry, Pollyanna?"

"The people on the right are away in Frisco on vacation. The house on the other side belongs to an old man named Stapleton. He lives alone with a fat old cocker spaniel."

"We'll drop in on Mr. Stapleton later."

"Watch out for that dog, he likes to nip at people."

"So do I on certain occasions," confided Groucho. "We'll have a lot in common."

We were heading for the kitchen when the police siren sounded outside.

Thirty-one

I knew Detective Gorman of the Manhattan Beach police from my *LA Times* days. He was in his early forties, overweight, and honest. He and his partner, a freckled, red-haired detective named Kendig, looked through Frances London's house, asked us all questions and told Polly that she should've called the police as soon as she suspected that her mother was missing.

Then, about a half hour after they'd arrived, Gorman pointed a thumb at me and then at the kitchen. "Want to talk to you, Frank."

"Care to have a witness along, Rollo?" inquired Groucho. He was sharing the sofa with a tearful Polly.

"It's all right," I assured him, stepping into the kitchen.

Closing the door, the detective roamed to a cookie jar shaped like a teddy bear. "You and Groucho pretending to be detectives again?" He lifted off the bear's head and dipped a hand into the jar. "Sugar cookies aren't my favorites." He extracted two.

"Groucho and I don't think Frances London killed anybody," I said, leaning against the sink. "We're trying to prove it."

He took a bite of one of the cookies. "How you coming?"

"Nothing yet, Ned, that we can turn over to the police." I

227

didn't want to tell him we might have a statement from Maggie Barnes tying Sergeant Branner in with the murder of Dr. Benninger. For one thing, I didn't know if the lawyer Groucho had dispatched to get the statement had succeeded.

"Where do you think Frances London is?" Opening the icebox, he looked inside. "Chocolate milk." He took the bottle out, held it up toward me. "Want any?"

"Nope," I said. "Suppose we can prove that there's a crooked cop involved in this whole mess?"

Detective Gorman found a glass in a cupboard, poured the chocolate milk. "Let me guess," he said. "You suspect that Sergeant Branner of the Bayside Police isn't completely honest."

"We suspect he's directly tied in to the Benninger killing."

The cop put the bottle away, took a sip of milk. "You're not a reporter anymore," he said, "so I guess I don't have to warn you not to quote me."

"Whatever you tell me, though, I'll share with Groucho."

He laughed. "I'm not especially afraid of any of the Marx Brothers," he said. "Branner is the worst kind of rotten cop and I'd like to see him knocked flat on his skinny ass."

"But?"

"Branner's got a lot of influential friends."

"Like Jack Cortez."

Nodding, Gorman finished his first sugar cookie. "You know what the setup is like in Bayside," he said. "Tartaglia, Cortez, Salermo, guys like that, pretty much tell the law what to do. If you came up with a technicolor movie showing Branner shooting a little old lady down in broad daylight and had a troop of Boy Scouts and six archbishops as backup witnesses, Branner would still get off. That is, if you turned your proof over to any of the top officials in Bayside."

"We weren't planning on doing that, Ned."

Gorman bit into the second cookie. "Some of the biggest crooks and conmen I know always start their spiels with 'You can trust me,' " he said. "But, Frank, you do know that you can trust me."

"I do, which is why I brought this up."

"You get anything tangible against Branner, give me a look and I'll see it gets to people who can do something about it." He looked directly at me. "What are you going for specifically?"

"Can't talk about it yet. But we'll have something soon."

"You think he killed Dr. Benninger?"

"He was definitely an accessory," I answered, "but it's more likely he was covering for some one else. He had a hand in framing Frances for the job."

Gorman wiped crumbs off his chin with the back of his hand. "What do you think happened here?"

"She was dragged off. Whoever did it wants everybody to think she's guilty and ran rather than face a trial."

"Let's say that is what happened. Any idea where they'd take her?"

"Not yet, no," I answered. "You and your partner have gone over the whole place—you don't believe she just packed up and took off, do you?"

He smiled and returned to the cookie jar. "Like the good policeman that I am, Frank, I'm keeping an open mind," he told me as he helped himself to another cookie.

"You never got around to telling me how you happened to show up here?"

"Got a phone call."

"Anonymous tip?"

"No, it was—"

"You no good son of a bitching bastard! Why'd you do that?"

Gorman frowned at the door. "Is that the kid yelling like that?"

"Yeah, it's Polly." I sprinted to the door and pulled it open.

What have I told you, young lady, about using that kind of language?" said Roger Pilgrim.

Polly hit her father in the face with her fisted hand, shouting, "You stupid asshole. You phoned them because you're trying to make her look guilty."

Putting both arms around her from behind, Groucho pulled her back out of range of Roger Pilgrim. "Let's get into a neutral corner, Battling Nelson."

The young singer struggled to break free for about thirty seconds, then subsided and began sobbing. "Now they're all going to think she's run away."

After dabbing at his cheek with his starchy pocket handkerchief, Pilgrim said, "I don't know why Frances left here, Polly," he said in his calm voice. "But the important thing, honey, is that she's disappeared. Whether she fled or whether she was abducted, I felt it was my duty—once I got your phone call telling me she was gone—to notify the police."

"We could've found her," said Polly. "Groucho and Frank and me. Now she's going to be labeled a fugitive and—"

"The police, as I'm sure even Groucho will concede, are better equipped to find missing persons."

As he escorted Polly back to the sofa and urged her, with a gentle pressure on her shoulder, to sit down, Groucho said, "Your pop's right, Pollyanna. Sooner or later we were probably going to have to contact the law ourselves."

"But because of him it's *sooner.*"

Detective Gorman told her, "Nobody's going to brand your mother anything, Miss Pilgrim. But we do want to locate her."

Polly looked at Groucho. "They shoot fugitives."

"Mostly in Warner Brothers epics." He settled beside her, patting her shoulder.

Her father asked Gorman, "In your opinion, officer, what happened?"

"Tough to tell, Mr. Pilgrim," he answered. "We'll have to get out an all-points bulletin on her. You check the garage yet, Kendig?"

The redheaded cop nodded. "Yeah, car's gone. I checked with Motor Vehicle and she's driving a thirty-four green Chevy sedan, license number 914JB18."

"I bet she isn't driving," said Polly. "Whoever kidnapped her stole her car, too."

"Even so, we still have to find the car."

Pilgrim cleared his throat. "Polly, I wonder if you'd go outside on the porch for a few minutes."

"I want to stay here."

"There are some things I have to talk over with the officers, not the sort of things I want you to hear."

"What does that mean? Haven't you done enough harm to her already?"

"Please, dear."

Groucho gave me a nod. "C'mon, Polly," I invited, "we'll go look around the neighborhood and see what we can find out."

"I earn more money than anyone in this room, except Groucho," she said, angry. "But I'm treated like a little kid whenever—"

"My family always shoos me out of the room when they

discuss anything serious," Groucho told her. "When a topic such as Albanian literature, solid geometry, or how to build a canoe comes up, it's 'Go to your room, Groucho.'" He stood. "Since my room happens to be in the Pasadena YMCA, it makes for a substantial hike every—"

"Okay, I'll go, Groucho. You don't have to humor me." She gave him a disappointed look and went out of the house.

When I caught up with her, she was standing forlornly on the porch.

Detective Gorman asked, "What was it you wanted to talk about, Mr. Pilgrim?"

After glancing toward the door, he said, "It upsets Polly whenever her mother's past life is discussed, officer. But, as you know, Frances was . . . well, promiscuous." He paused. "I wanted to know if there was any indication that there was a man staying here with her."

"None."

"And nothing to suggest a sexual encounter?"

"That's right."

Pilgrim sighed out a breath. "I was concerned that Frances might have picked up someone at a bar and brought him home," he explained. "In the past, some of her escapades in that direction led to violence."

"She didn't have a guest here last night, far as we can tell."

He looked again toward the doorway. "I talked to my ex-wife, briefly, last evening when—"

"What time was that?" asked Gorman.

"Somewhere around nine."

"So she was still here then," the detective said.

"What I was about to tell you, officer, was that Frances sounded extremely depressed," Pilgrim continued. "There were, as you probably know, at least two suicide attempts in the past. Is there anything pointing to the possibility that she intended to harm herself in any way?"

"She didn't leave a suicide note behind, if that's what you mean."

"That's good news," said Pilgrim. "Although it doesn't rule out suicide."

"Why, pray tell, would she kill herself?" inquired Groucho.

"I'd like to be as optimistic as Polly is," said her father. "Even though I put up Frances's bail and arranged for an attorney, I'm not completely convinced that she didn't actually kill Dr. Benninger while she was drunk. Feeling guilty and wanting to spare us the pain of a trial, she might well—"

"Frances didn't kill that quack," Groucho assured him. "And, by the way, remind me not to come to you the next time I'm in need of a character reference."

"It's fine to humor an unhappy young girl," said Pilgrim, "but I believe in facing reality."

"You're facing in the wrong direction this time." Groucho took a fresh cigar from his jacket pocket, crossing the room. "I do believe I'll go outside and see if I can scare up a rousing game of kick the can."

Thirty-two

I hadn't anticipated that as the day faded that Jane and I would be driving to the town of Cottonville out in the San Fernando Valley. All because of a hunch of Groucho's.

When he and I had asked questions of the neighbors of Frances London, we learned that no one had seen or heard the Ford leaving her garage between the time Pilgrim said he'd talked to her on the telephone the night before and the time her daughter found she was missing the next morning. Old Mr. Stapleton, however, swore he'd seen Roger Pilgrim's peach-colored limousine draw up in front of France's place at about 11:00 P.M. He'd turned in right after that, so he didn't know how long the car'd been there.

Polly told us both her father and his chauffeur had left the mansion at about ten the night before, but she had no idea where they went nor exactly when they got home. She was all for going in and demanding that her father tell her what he'd been up to.

"Although I'm not noted for my subtlety," Groucho told her, "I think we'd be better served if we kept mum about what we've found out. Then later, Mum can keep us."

"You think my father had something to do with what's happened to her?"

"I think, child, that he was doing a very good job of trying to make her look bad in the eyes of the law when the gumshoes were talking to him."

"So do I," said the young singer. "That's why I slugged him."

We were standing on the sidewalk down the block from Frances's house by this time. Groucho halted and produced a fresh cigar. "Besides your palatial mansion, Pollyanna," he inquired as he lit the stogie, "does your pappy have any other houses hereabouts? Hideaway cottages, flats, mountain cabins?"

"There's that place in the Valley," she answered. "It's in Cottonville, near that old Western movie location. They have meetings there sometimes, when my father wants privacy. And once in a while, an out-of-town client stays there."

"Eureka," observed Groucho and asked her for the address. "Rollo, I would appreciate it if you go take a look at that choice patch of real estate."

"You think my mother's there?" asked Polly, fists clenching. "Then we better go in right now and face my father and—"

"What I'm suffering from now, kiddo" he explained, "is just a hunch. But I think we ought to look into it."

"But maybe we don't have all that much time to—"

"There's time," he said. "Can you undertake this chore, Frank?"

I nodded, saying, "Sure, but what—"

"Since I'm a great believer in the latest criminology equipment, Rollo, I'll try to arrange to have an old acquaintance of yours help out on this escapade."

"You're going to be doing what while I'm—"

"I'll be playing the bait in a trap." He exhaled smoke. "In

order to facilitate that, I'd be awfully pleased if you'd plant a bit of information with some of your underworld informants and suggest that they circulate it far and wide."

"What bit of information?"

"The present whereabouts of Maggie Barnes."

As my Plymouth went bumping along a side road in Cottonville, I said, "This may not be too safe, Jane, and—"

"If you're going to get killed, Frank, I think I ought to be around," said Jane from the passenger seat. "That's what devotion is all about."

"True," I admitted. "But I wasn't talking about getting knocked off, only roughed up some. Once we get there, you should probably stay in the car and—"

"No, I intend to tag along." She reached out and put her hand on my shoulder. "I'll help you load the muskets and all the other things dutiful females do in situations such as this. Do you think Frances London really is being held at Pilgrim's hideaway?"

"Well, it seems like a strong possibility," I answered, slowly. "I do agree with Groucho that Pilgrim seemed to be setting up a suicide for Frances when he was talking to Detective Gorman in Manhattan Beach this morning."

"That doesn't mean the guy grabbed her out of her house, dragged up here, and is going to fake the suicide himself," Jane pointed out. "Could be he simply wanted to make her look bad to the cops."

"That's true," I agreed, slowing the car. "What I'm really looking into is Groucho's hunch that she might be here."

Up ahead on the road loomed a high redwood fence. Above the wide gate was a weathered sign that announced—Cotton-

237

ville Ranch. Where some of the greatest western motion pictures of all time were filmed! Duke Cotton, proprietor.

"I didn't know Hoot Gibson and Ken Maynard made some of the great Western motion pictures of all time," mentioned Jane as I guided the car through the open gateway and stopped on the false-front main street.

"Well, not as great as Bob Steele probably," I said. "This used to be a thriving location for B movies, though."

"I'm aware of that," she said, "which is why I mentioned Ken Maynard."

"Howdy." A tall, lanky man in Levi's, plaid shirt, and scuffed cowboy boots had come strolling over to the car. He removed his low-crown Stetson with a sweeping gesture and bowed in Jane's direction. "Right pleased to meet up with you, Missy. You're mighty pretty. I'm Duke Cotton."

It was indeed the cowboy star of silent movies, older and grayer than in his heyday.

I said, "Groucho Marx was going to arrange with you for us to—"

"Yep, he sure enough did. You're interested in one of my neighbor's, huh?"

"The Roger Pilgrim setup, yeah."

Cotton nodded. "And you're Frank Denby?"

"I am and this is Jane Danner."

"Not hitched up?" He bowed again. "Welcome to the Cottonville Ranch, miss. If you'll park this buggy over front of the saloon yonder, Frank, I'll point you in the direction of the Pilgrim spread."

"Groucho was also supposed to—"

"Yep, that's all took care of, too. I'll go fetch the critter whiles you're parking."

"Critter?" inquired Jane as we drove along the dusty road and parked near the hitching rail in front of the Golden Bear Saloon.

"I was keeping it as a surprise." Turning off the engine, I got out and went around to open her door. "Groucho hired Dorgan for us again."

She smiled. "That cute bloodhound we used when you fellows were working on the Peg McMorrow case."

"The same."

"He helped us find a body and . . ." He voice faded, along with her smile. "You think Frances is buried out there someplace?"

"Nope," I said. "Dorgan finds live people, too, remember?"

A yelping commenced off in the gathering dusk.

"Whoa there, fella," said Cotton.

Dorgan, yelping in a pleased way, came running in his wobbly fashion toward us.

He threw himself enthusiastically, sending a cloud of dust swirling up, at Jane's feet. Then he rolled over on his back, panting happily.

She bent and rubbed at his gray belly with the palm of her hand. "A pleasure meeting you again, Dorgan."

He rolled from side to side, tongue lolling, panting.

"His trainer dropped him off here about half an hour ago," explained the cowboy actor. "He's been fretting ever since, must've known you folks were going to drop by."

Kneeling, Jane took hold of the bloodhound's leash. "Should we get going, Frank?"

"In a minute." Opening the rumble seat of the Plymouth, I fetched out a flashlight and the paper bag I'd acquired at Frances London's house.

"You in the picture business?" Cotton asked Jane.

"No." Standing up, she brushed dust from her tan slacks. "C'mon, Dorgan."

Tugging at his leash, the bloodhound waddled over to me. He rose up on his hind legs and planted his forepaws against my groin.

I patted him on the head, set him on the ground again. "We've got another job for you, Dorgan," I informed him while he licked my hand. From the paper bag I took the blouse that Groucho had smuggled out of Frances's closet. "This is who we're looking for."

The dog devoted himself to giving the blouse a thorough sniffing. Raising his head, he then took a whiff of the night air.

"You can stick around here, miss," invited the lean cowboy actor. "Lot of brambles and nettles in that there woods."

"Thanks, but Dorgan and I consider ourselves a team."

The bloodhound, making small whimpering noises, was pulling against the leash, eager to head into the woods.

"Where exactly is the Pilgrim place?" I asked Cotton.

He pointed toward the darkening forest that rose up just to the rear of the movie town's main street. "Due south down that there way, Frank, for maybe a mile," he said. "You'll come to a clearing with high hedges around it. Other side of them is a big redwood house as well as a garage, two sheds and three cottages. Looks to me like that dog's going to lead you just about there anyway."

"Let's go," Jane said to Dorgan.

He made a pleased sound and headed for the woods.

"Good hunting, folks," called Cotton.

The bloodhound was pulling Jane after him on a zigzag path downhill. I turned on the flash and followed them.

"In case," said Jane over her shoulder to me, "you ever have reason to doubt my attractiveness, remember Duke Cotton."

"Shucks, he was just being courteous. That's the code of the West."

"Where's it say in the code of the West that you pat ladies on their backsides?"

I slowed. "Did that son of a bitch try to—"

"Don't fret, I was able to dissuade him."

"Even so, I—"

"Let's concentrate on where Dorgan is leading us."

I was silent for a few minutes, mad.

Dorgan, panting methodically, was heading to what might actually be due south. I was never very good on south, north, and directions like that. Left and right I'd pretty much mastered.

"Lights showing up ahead," I said, clicking off my flashlight. "That could be the house."

"Slow down a little, Dorgan," Jane suggested to the eager bloodhound, pulling on his leash.

Reluctantly, he slowed his descent through the brush and between the oaks and walnut trees.

We could see the main house now. It was a two-story red-wood structure and there was light showing at several windows on the ground floor. There were also lights on in one of the cottages.

Dorgan was making small whimpering sounds, hunching his shoulders, tugging at the restraining leash.

"Let's see," I suggested, "where he wants to go."

Jane patted the dog on his side, saying softly, "Okay, lead on, Dorgan."

He wound his way through the trees, head low. He lead us clear of the woods at a spot behind the main house. Then, finding a break in one of the hedges, he moved onto the grounds of the Pilgrim property.

Darkness had closed in by now and there was no moonlight yet.

The bloodhound ignored the house, went trotting toward the cottage where the light was showing.

I couldn't see anybody on the grounds, no one anywhere near the small shingled house. Very carefully we moved closer.

Hunched low, I eased up to the window and risked a look inside.

Frances London was in the living room, sitting up straight in a wood and leather armchair.

And standing close to her, a .32 revolver in his hand, was Roger Pilgrim.

They were talking, but none of the conversation got out of the room.

At my side Dorgan suddenly made a growling sound.

Then behind me someone said, "Evening, Frankie."

Thirty-three

Maggie Barnes scowled in Groucho's direction. "Why'd you bring that thing with you?"

Hugging his guitar to him in a sort of maternal way, he answered, "We may have a long night ahead of us, my dear. Music helps while away the time."

"Not my time." She was sitting on the rustic sofa in the large, beam-ceilinged living room of the house where she'd been kept hidden away ever since she and Groucho had jumped out of the window of the bordello. "I'm kind of starting to think I was a sap to go along with you on this latest brainstorm of yours."

"You're perfectly safe, Mag." He was perched on the edge of a rustic wood and leather armchair and he put his guitar on his knee and strummed a few chords. "Would you like to hear a medley of old Nick Lucas favorites? I've had oodles of compliments on my rendition of 'Tiptoe Through the Tulips.'"

"Nick Lucas was a sissy."

"Well then, how about my rendition of 'Tiptoe Through the Pansies'?"

The blonde produced a disdainful noise. "You might as well play a funeral march, since we're both going to get killed." She left the sofa and walked over to the draped front windows. "There's probably already a whole gang of them out there will tommy guns."

"But that's precisely what we want," he reminded. "That's how a trap works. You place the bait at point A. and then the quarry appears at point B. and moves toward point A. At which time—"

"They shoot us full of holes." Maggie reached out to part the drapes, then decided she didn't want to look out into the darkness beyond the house. Instead she returned to the sofa, sat down hard, folded her arms under her breasts. "I gave that skinflint lawyer of yours my statement, Groucho, and that should've been enough."

"It's a step in the right direction," he conceded. "But we can also use more direct evidence."

"How about my lifeless corpse chock-full of bullet holes? That direct enough?" She shook her blond head. "Like I told you, Groucho, I'm sorry I agreed to this half-assed plan of yours."

"Frankly, Maggie, I was growing impatient," he said. "I'm hoping this'll nudge them into tripping themselves up."

"Yeah, and knocking us off in the process."

"If it works, you'll be safe. Free to come and go as you—"

"Swell," she said. "Then I can go back to being a hooker and have the time of my life. I can sleep with a bunch of assholes and not have a care in the world."

"You won't have to return to that particular mode of employment."

"So what do I do instead? Strap on some roller skates and work as a car hop in some half-baked drive-in out in Pomona?"

"Actually, the chain of half-baked drive-ins I have influence with only operates out of Oxnard. However, one of the advantages of working for them is that you get to keep the roller skates. Plus you get all the french fries you can—"

"Level with me, Groucho," the young woman cut in. "If I don't end up in Forest Lawn after tonight, are you really going to help me get work?"

"I've already begun the process," he assured her. "As soon as the coast is clear, we'll start rolling. Ah, but keep in mind that we're referring here to the coast of Yucatán, which usually requires just an awful lot of work to clear. In fact, the last time we tried to clear it, why, all the king's horses, all the king's men and the entire outfield of a Japanese baseball team took days and days to—"

"Does your wife ever get fed up with your kidding around all the time?"

"Frequently, yes," he admitted. "Matter of fact, I'm already on my second wife. I wore the first one down to a nub with my jocularity and frivolous remarks. I imagine that—"

At the moment he was interrupted by the front door being booted open.

Gesturing at Jane with his .45 automatic, Pilgrim's chauffeur ordered, "Keep that damn mutt quiet."

Jane knelt on the hooked rug and patted the growling, grumbling Dorgan on his side. "Hush up, boy," she suggested, "or the lout's liable to shoot you."

The dog made a shuddering movement and quieted down.

"That's enough of that kind of talk, lady."

"Careful," I told her. "It's not a good idea to insult louts. Particularly armed louts who—"

"Unfortunately, Frank," said Pilgrim, "you seem to have

picked up some of Groucho's inappropriate flippancy."

"It has nothing to do with Groucho." Jane straightened up. "He's been this way since birth."

Pilgrim was standing directly behind the chair Frances London was sitting in. "None of this is particularly funny, Miss Danner."

"He's going to have to kill you, too," said the blond actress. "After he gets finished arranging my suicide."

"C'mon," I said to Pilgrim, "you can't get away with a multiple suicide. I doubt if even crooked cops will—"

"You two will be having an automobile accident," Pilgrim informed me. "Afraid that Frances was planning to take her life, you came rushing up here in that unsafe little car of yours. In your haste you misjudged a dangerous curve and . . ." He shrugged, smiled thinly. "Egon will arrange the details."

After a few seconds I realized that Egon must be the chauffeur. Up until now nobody had ever bothered to introduce the guy to me.

"That'll make Egon a murderer," said Jane.

"That doesn't bother me, lady."

"Roger's been trying to get me to sign a suicide note, confessing to the murder," Frances told us and touching at a red spot on her cheek.

"Eventually you're going to sign the note," her former husband promised. "A farewell letter, confessing all and expressing profound guilt over what you've done. That will add a convincing touch."

"A little flaw there," I mentioned. "She didn't kill the doctor."

"No one's ever likely to establish that."

"Groucho is," I told him. "Probably tonight."

Pilgrim stroked his chin with his free hand. "It might be better then to have Frances kill herself simply out of remorse over all the trouble she's caused us."

"I'm never going to sign a damn thing."

Pilgrim said, "We'll persuade you. In ways that won't leave any traces."

I asked him, "This will be your first killing, won't it? The way Groucho and I have figured this out, Dr. Benninger was—"

"It really doesn't matter," said Egon, "what you guys think."

"No, I appreciate their interest." Pilgrim pointed his revolver at me. "You don't believe I killed the doctor—then what am I up to here, Frank?"

"Well, despite your look of affluence and financial stability," I said, "you're really like one of those old West towns. Nothing much behind the false front."

"You writers certainly have a gift for lively expressions."

I moved a step closer to the sprawled dog. "Actually, Pilgrim, you're in hock to some mean-minded gamblers."

"So that's the reason," murmured Frances.

"The money Polly's going to get from that new Paragon Pictures contract is going to save your neck," I continued. "Sure, I know there are laws to protect the incomes of kid stars, but you're shrewd enough to get around those. You've probably already promised Salermo's boys that you'll be sharing the wealth with them until your debt's canceled."

Frances looked up at her former husband, shaking her head. "He's worried because Polly and I are close again."

"Yep, Pilgrim's afraid she'll want to use her money to help you out," I said. "And also that if you and Polly stay friendly, you're going to find out he's tangled up with a lot of prominent mobsters. You'd be able to get the court to return custody of your daughter to you."

"He did take care of my bail and—"

"More front. He wanted to look good, so nobody'd suspect what he was really up to," I said, easing nearer to the dormant Dorgan. "But he got a little too eager to make you look like a potential suicide and it got Groucho to wondering."

"What the hell is this," asked the annoyed Egon, "the god-damned Gettysburg Address?"

"The Gettysburg Address is much shorter," said Jane.

"So this is all about Polly's money," said Frances.

"Money's a very popular motive."

The actress asked me, "You don't think he had anything to do with killing Russ Benninger?"

"Nope, he just took advantage of your getting tangled up in the murder," I replied.

"If I'm going to rig a fake accident with that jalopy of his," said Egon, "I better get started."

"First things first," said Pilgrim. We have to take care of Frances."

"Too many people know bout this place. I think—"

I nudged Dorgan hard in his backside with the toe of my shoe.

The bloodhound yelped, shot straight up, and then lunged for the chauffeur's leg.

I lunged, too, and managed to grab the startled Egon's gun hand before he could use his automatic.

I spun him around, getting him between me and Pilgrim.

Jane meantime had dived to the floor and scooted behind a table.

Next came two shots.

Pilgrim made a strange gurgling sound. He raised his gun up chest high, then dropped it. The front of his suit coat was growing bloody. He fell to the floor just in front of his former wife's feet.

"Good thing I came on down here to look around," said Duke Cotton from the open front doorway. He held a six-gun in each hand. "I kept that varmint from shooting you all up." He glanced over at Jane. "You all right, miss?"

"I'm fine." She got up. "Thanks."

"Better let go of your gun, Egon," I told the chauffeur.

We'd been struggling for possession during the shooting.

"Shit," he complained and released his grip on the automatic.

Thirty-four

The short, handsome Jack Cortez smiled at Groucho. "You must be one of the few guys left who brings a guitar along when he shacks up with a broad," he observed.

"Music hath charms." Groucho stood up and carefully leaned the instrument against the chair he'd been sitting in. "Which is more than I can say for either you or your sidekick. And if anybody ever needed a good swift kick in the side, it's you, Sergeant Branner."

The thin cop, cigarette in one knobby hand and .38 revolver in the other, had followed the mobster from out of the night into the living room. "This is what comes from playing detective, Julius," he said. "I warned you about fooling around with this case."

Groucho glanced up at the beamed ceiling. "I know, sarge, but playing detective is so much more fun than playing Monopoly or even playing the harmonium, that I couldn't resist. My brother Chico feels the same way about playing the horses. When I was asked to play a horse, though, I turned them down because they didn't offer me the leading part. I, therefore—"

"Suppose you shut up." Cortez shut the door and moved

farther into the room.

"That's an interesting motion. Is there a second?"

Branner said, "You're forgetting, Jack, that this guy thinks he's a comedian. Let him have one last fling."

Maggie had started crying softly. "He made me come here, sergeant," she told him, sniffling into a lace-trimmed hankie. "I couldn't do a damn thing about it. But, I swear, I haven't told him anything."

"At this point it really doesn't matter, Maggie," said the cop.

"But you can trust me not to blab. You don' have to—"

"We do have to, honey," said the policeman. "Let me explain the scenario to you, so you'll understand your part in it."

"If it's all the same with you guys," she said, "I'd like to retire from acting right about now."

"It's a very simple part." Branner rested his free hand on the arm of her chair, leaned close, and exhaled smoke. "See, this is a love nest we've discovered here."

"I'm not an especially critical person," put in Groucho, "but I would like to point out that you're lacking some of the essential ingredients for a first-class love nest."

"We've got all we need." The cop kept his eyes on the tearful blonde. "We've got a well-known whore and a dirty old man. Perfect setup."

"I deeply resent being alluded to as a dirty old man," complained Groucho. "A dirty middle-aged man perhaps, yet not—"

"Shut up," advised Cortez. From his shoulder holster he produced an automatic.

"Well, when you put it that way," said Groucho.

Branner backed away from Maggie. "Groucho, as the story will go, developed this obsessive passion for you, Maggie. He broke into Mrs. Ferguson's joint and dragged you off against your will. Plenty of witnesses to that. He kept you a prisoner here and, when you refused to give in to his perverse sexual suggestions, he threatened you with a gun. You struggled and in that unfortunate struggle, the gun went off—twice. Killed you both." His shook his head in mock sadness.

"Colossal," remarked Groucho. "Who do you see in the role of Groucho?"

"Let's get this started," suggested Cortez.

Holding his right hand in a wait-a-minute gesture, Groucho said, "I guess this is the end of the trail, Branner. And, as you prophesied, my trying to be a detective has brought me to an ignominious end, whatever that might be."

"Yeah, so?" said the impatient Cortez.

To the cop Groucho said, "I developed a theory, even though I'm only an amateur at this game, and . . ." He paused to sigh a forlorn sigh. "Well, shucks, before I take off for Glory, could you satisfy my curiosity?"

Cortez said, "Let's just shoot them and—"

"What was it you wanted to know, Julius?"

"Why are we wasting time with this bullshit?" demanded Cortez.

"It's my last request," Groucho pointed out. "Law officers have to honor those. You're lucky I didn't also order a pastrami sandwich and a blueberry knish for my last meal. Or the services of a rabbi."

"We can spare a few minutes," Branner told the gangster.

After another glance toward the ceiling, Groucho said, "I truly appreciate this, Branner, and I've come to the realization, albeit a bit late in the game, that you're not quite as rotten a rat as I'd originally surmised."

"What's your theory?" asked the sergeant.

"It all began with Brian Montaine," said Groucho, raising his voice some. "He was still in love with his wife—one more proof of the saying that there's no accounting for taste. All right, the deluded hambone was still enamored of Dianne Sayler and he vowed that, to win her back, he was going to kick the dope habit for good and all. To help him reach his goal, Montaine intended to make his addiction public. That would probably finish him in the movie business, but since he possessed a nest egg of massive proportions, he didn't care about that. As part of his plan he meant to tell all he knew about the Tartaglia-Cortez drug operations and about the interesting role Dr. Benninger was playing. Now, granted, several important cops in the Los Angeles area, including you, Branner, already knew all about that but were being paid to pretend otherwise." Groucho paused, cleared his throat, and continued. "However, if Montaine made a public confession, then *everybody* would know. It would be in all the newspapers, *Time* would give it a cover story, all the trade papers would write it up, Johnny Whistler would devote two or three minutes to it on his radio show. Even in a state as corrupt as California, there would have to be an investigation. The federals would come in on it, too."

"Okay, you're right so far," admitted Branner.

"One of you fellows got wind of what Brian Montaine was planning to do," said Groucho. "Probably because he confided in a few too many of his friends and one of them—"

"I found out about it," said Cortez. "Now can we—"

"Relax, Jack," Branner advised his colleague. "Go on, Groucho."

"You went to Dr. Benninger—that was probably you, sergeant—and told him what the celluloid King Arthur was going to do," Groucho went on. "You told him to drop in on his longtime client and give him what is known in the trade as a hot shot. We know Benninger telephoned Montaine on the night the actor died. Probably he told him he had to come over and talk to him, maybe even suggested that he was ready to tell what he knew, too. The two of them could go to the papers with the story. So Montaine, all alone in his mansion, let the doctor in. Benninger sapped him and gave him the fatal hypo."

Branner lit a fresh cigarette from the butt of the old one. "That's pretty much, sure, what happened."

"The doctor, though, was very upset by the whole business." Groucho locked his hands behind his back and commenced pacing. "He started fretting even before he did the deed, but you leaned on him enough to make him go ahead. Afterward, he felt even worse. You began to worry that he'd crack, too, and start talking. You didn't want that, so you arranged a death for him and—"

"Enough of this crap," cut in Cortez. "I helped Branner get rid of Benninger. The bastard was feeling, for Christ sake, guilty. And he was drinking even more than usual. We had to keep him quiet and killing him was the simplest way. Now can we get on with this?"

Groucho nodded in the sergeant's direction. "Why frame Frances London for the job?"

"She was convenient," he answered with a shrug. "She used to date Benninger, they'd just had a public squabble at the Troc. She had a nice reputation for getting drunk and doing violent things and, just as I figured, nobody would believe her story that she was on the wagon now and had been set up. Oh, and I never much liked her either."

"You hired Maggie here to help build the frame," said Groucho, indicating the blonde with his thumb.

"Didn't she already tell you that?" He smiled his thin smile again. "I knew Maggie and I was aware she looked something like the London dame. I wanted some honest witnesses to testify that they'd seen Frances London hammering on the doctor's door and threatening to break in."

"And Benninger was already dead when Maggie staged her charade?"

"Sure, we'd already taken care of him," said Branner.

"And you'd already conned Frances into driving out to a job interview, where some of your goons were waiting."

"Some of Jack's goons," corrected the cop. "They're good at that sort of thing. Knock a dame out, give her a shot to keep her asleep, pour booze into her through a rubber tube. They're craftsmen."

Groucho went over to stand near Maggie's chair. "Anything further you'd like to state, my dear?"

"Nope, you've summed it up great, Groucho," the blonde said, tucking her handkerchief away in the front of her dress. "Except I might add that after tonight's performance, I think I ought to be considered for radio work."

Branner scowled. "What in the hell are you two babbling about?"

Groucho now used his thumb to point at the beamed ceiling. "There's a microphone planted up there, sarge," he explained. "Borrowed from the Nationwide Broadcasting Network, along with two technicians from that popular comedy hit, *Groucho Marx, Private Eye,* and installed under the supervision of our talented director, Annie Nicola."

"You son of a bitch." Cortez jabbed his gun at the air separating him from Groucho. "You been broadcasting this over the radio?"

"Not exactly, Jack. We've merely been making an electrical transcription."

"Then let's have that damn transcription so we can—"

"The disk is in a studio several miles from here," explained Groucho. "This delightful conversation was sent along the airwaves to the recording studio, where it now resides safely. A wonderful feature of these transcriptions, fellows, is that they can be played many, many times and give hours of pleasure to—"

"We may not have the record," said Branner, "but we've got you and Maggie."

"You do, true," admitted Groucho. "But what we've got, waiting silently and patiently in the master bedroom and elsewhere, is a select group of policemen. They are all, to a man, armed and honest."

Cortez said, "Bullshit, we didn't see any cars anywhere around here or—"

"Most of them are former Boy Scouts," Groucho said. "After hiding their police vehicles at a respectable distance, they snuck silently over here quite awhile ago." He took a cigar from his coat pocket, unwrapped it, and lighted it with a wood match. "It would be a good idea if you would both surrender your weapons."

Cortez said, "It's a bluff."

The bedroom door opened halfway and someone said, "It isn't a bluff, Jack."

Branner tossed his gun on a chair. "Don't worry, Jack, we'll get out of this," he said.

"Transcription," muttered Cortez and dropped his gun to the floor.

Groucho took a puff on his cigar. "I saw Chester Morris pull a trick like this in a B movie once," he confided in Maggie. "But I really wasn't sure it would work in real life."

Thirty-five

That Tuesday afternoon's rehearsal turned out to be a memorable one.

Polly Pilgrim showed up in jeans and an old sweatshirt. "I've decided I'm not ready to be glamorous," she told me when I joined her on the studio stage. "So no more fancy clothes for rehearsals, Frank. My mother agrees with me, too. She also told me that she was gawky and overweight when she was my age."

"Most everybody was."

"Oh, I don't think Myrna Loy was."

"One of the few possible exceptions. You're living with Frances now?"

"Yes, and it's swell," the young singer answered. "I'm staying at her place in Manhattan Beach while she gets all her things packed and ready to move and then she'll come and live with me in the mansion."

"Looks like your father and your chauffeur are going to be charged with kidnapping and several related infractions."

"I hope they send them both up the river for a good long stretch."

"That's likely what'll happen."

"Good," she said. "I'm having some men crate up all his things and haul them away. My idea was to have them dump the crates way out in the Pacific Ocean, but my mother says I should just have them put in storage." She made a face. "I wouldn't mind, if you want to know, putting my father in a crate and dumping him somewhere."

"Best thing to do is—"

"Groucho." She'd noticed him loping along the aisle and leaped free of her folding chair. She ran down the steps and started for him.

He dropped his guitar case before she got both arms around him in an enthusiastic hug.

"Usually it's two falls out of three," Groucho gasped, "but I'm willing to concede the match right now."

"I just wanted to thank you again," Polly told him, relaxing her hug. "I'm really happy now, Groucho, and my mother and I are together, and I—"

"If you don't want to get hauled away for suffocating aging troubadours, Pollyanna, ease up on the death grip."

She laughed, letting go of him. Then she noticed the guitar case. "You're not going to sing any Gilbert and Sullivan on our show, are you, Groucho? Our Hooper ratings are awful enough now without—"

"Fear not, little princess," He crouched and retrieved the guitar. "I am merely going to warble a jingle that Frank and I whipped up. It extols the virtues of all five flavorful flavors of Mullens pudding and all and sundry who've heard it agree that it will add plenty of new zing to our broadcasts. As you may recall from our last episode, Old Zing had fallen in the well along with Tiny Bobby the lame tap dancer from the Old Sod, and—"

"As long as it's not Gilbert and Sullivan." She darted, kissed him on the cheek and ran back onto the stage.

"Being the object of your affection, child, is a challenging job," he informed her as he sat down two chairs over from me. "You are no doubt aware, Rollo, that for many years psychical investigators have struggled to communicate successfully with the dead."

"I was aware of that, Groucho, yes."

"It may interest you to know that less than an hour ago I accomplished an equally difficult feat," he announced. "Yes, strange as it may seem, I was able to carry on a coherent conversation with an advertising executive."

"One of those guys from BBD and O?"

"You don't have to spell out things in front of little Polly," Groucho said. "She's surely heard the word *bubbadeeoh* before, since these days young people use all sorts of foul language on the playground and in the—"

"Which adman did you talk to?"

"Buzz Hodges it was who telephoned me from far off Manhattan."

"What'd he say?"

Groucho took a fresh cigar from the pocket of his maize-colored checkered sport coat. "Because of all the mentions of *Groucho Marx, Private Eye* that have appeared in the yellow press across this vast land of ours after you and I solved the Benninger case, he thinks our ratings will climb without any further tinkering. So we don't have to make any changes whatsoever in our radio show until further notice."

"That's great," I said, grinning. "And Colonel Mullens agrees?"

"Apparently so," answered Groucho. "There are rumors that some of his more disgruntled employees heaved the old gent into a vat of his own butterscotch pudding. When he surfaced he was speaking with such a distinct Highland accent that he was relieved of his command and put to work in the shipping room. The particular ship they assigned him was the *Lusitania* and—"

Polly said, "You're in an awfully silly mood today, Groucho."

"You've noticed it, too? I suspect it has something to do with that earthquake in Mexico."

"They haven't," she said, "had an earthquake in Mexico recently."

"Well, there you are," he said, unwrapping the cigar. "We sent out well over a hundred invitations to our nearest and dearest friends stating, 'Drop over to the Marx hacienda for an After the Mexican Earthquake Party.' How do you think I must feel when you tell me there was no earthquake? The answer, little girl, is lopsided and covered with polka dots."

"Frank," said our director, Annie Nicola, from the booth. "Pick up the phone down there. You've got an emergency call."

"Jesus, what's wrong?" I sprinted over to the small table that held the phone and grabbed up the receiver. "Hello?"

"You sound distressed," said Jane.

"Are you okay? Were you in an accident? Are you sick?"

"Is this one of those multiple choice things?"

"Annie said it was an emergency call so I assumed—"

"Sorry, but the switchboard girl told me they couldn't put me through to you unless it was an emergency."

"Okay, so what's the real purpose of your call?"

"I've reached an important decision," she said. "And I didn't feel I wanted to wait until you came home to tell you."

"Is this something that's going to cause me to walk into the ocean fully clothed and never return?"

"Didn't they already do that in *A Star Is Born*?" she said. "No, this is, far as I can tell, good news."

"Okay. What?"

"I think I actually made this decision the other night when we almost got killed again," Jane began. "Let's get married before we move into the new place."

I laughed. "That's great. And you're sure?"

"Absolutely, which is another first for me."

"I accept your proposal," I said, laughing again. "We'll work out the details tonight."

"I'm happy," she said and hung up.

I walked back over to Groucho. "Well," I said, grinning.

"What did you win?"

"Jane and I. We're going to get married. Right now."

"Could you possibly wait until the rehearsal is over?"

"I mean, you know, before we move in together. Any day now. Momentarily."

Standing up, he shook my hand. "This is likely to be the only serious thing I'm going to say for the rest of the week, Frank," he said. "But congratulations. She's a splendid girl and far too good for the likes of you."

"Would you be our best man?"

He blew out smoke. "Well, I was sort of hoping to be the flower girl," Groucho said. "Still and all, I suppose I can settle for best man."